THE
BUZZARD GUNS

Center Point
Large Print

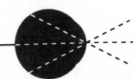

**This Large Print Book carries the
Seal of Approval of N.A.V.H.**

THE BUZZARD GUNS

Philip Ketchum

CENTER POINT LARGE PRINT
THORNDIKE, MAINE

Library of Congress Cataloging-in-Publication Data

Names: Ketchum, Philip, 1902–1969, author.
Title: The buzzard guns / Philip Ketchum.
Description: Center Point Large Print edition. | Thorndike, Maine :
Center Point Large Print, 2017.
Identifiers: LCCN 2016056407| ISBN 9781683243199 (hardcover : alk.
paper) | ISBN 9781683243236 (pbk. : alk. paper)
Subjects: LCSH: Large type books. | GSAFD: Western stories.
Classification: LCC PS3521.E835 B89 2017 | DDC 813/.52—dc23
LC record available at https://lccn.loc.gov/2016056407

THE
BUZZARD GUNS

CHAPTER 1

It had been a long ride, a ride that had covered more miles than Jeff Carmody wanted to remember. It had consumed three months' time—wasted time. Or perhaps it hadn't been wasted. He had felt restless. He had wanted a change, an opportunity to get away for a while. He had wanted to see different people, new scenes. And he had done it. Maybe now he could go home, settle down again and fall into the old routines.

He was frowning now, not at all pleased with his thoughts. What was it that made a man restless, that drove him to break his patterns, that left him uneasy, unsure, feeling incomplete? In his own case, there had been an incident to spark his departure, but, as tragic as it had been, his own trouble went deeper. Grandy had sensed it, too, and had encouraged him to leave. He had said, "Jeff, you're getting so you're not worth a damn. You've been working too hard and too long. Now you're thinking of getting married. That'll double your job. Before you do it, take a trip. Do a little helling. Get it out of your system."

Jeff wasn't sure how much helling he had done, and he wasn't sure his restlessness was gone, but, at least now, on his way home, he was looking forward to the next day. Maybe there was his answer. He wanted to get home. It would be good to drop down into the Park again.

He had had dinner at Indian Bluff, and now, late in the afternoon, he was climbing high into the mountains, following the pass road. By dusk he would make the stage station at Armand's Fork, where he could have supper. After that he would keep on, topping the pass. By morning he would be in the Park.

He paused briefly to have a cigarette, his thoughts on the next day. It would be nice to see Grandy again. It would even please him to see Wade and Syl. And, of course, Vicki. She had been bitter toward him the last time he saw her, but that was understandable. Her brother's death had been a shock. It took a little time to get over a thing like that.

Jeff was a tall young man, sharp-featured, deeply tanned. The past three months had thinned his face, but his body was solid, wiry-muscled, and he had wide shoulders. His eyes were dark, and at the moment he looked worried. He had a number of regrets, but regrets didn't help. The past couldn't be rewritten. People had to live with it.

He rode on, climbing higher. The sun went down. Light faded from the sky, and darkness came. He was near Armand's Fork, however, and soon he made it, pulling into the yard. There was no stage in sight and he expected no guests inside, but when he went in he noticed two men at the small table with Scroggins, the station agent. They had been playing blackjack, but as he entered they stopped and looked around. Scroggins, the only one Jeff recognized, looked startled to see him for some reason.

Jeff nodded. "Howdy, Scroggins. Anything left to eat?"

"I—I guess so," Scroggins said, gulping.

One of the other two men looked about forty. He was average-sized, and he might have been a cowhand traveling the pass. He needed a shave and probably could have used a bath. The other man was younger, near Jeff's age. He had sharp, clear eyes and rusty hair. He seemed to be smiling, but for no particular reason. He wore the same kind of clothing as his companion, but his shirt looked clean and his hands weren't grimy.

Scroggins got to his feet. He was a short, thick-bodied man, and he wore a full beard. He shouted, "Hey, Mom. Warm up some food."

A very small woman looked in from the kitchen. She looked tired, and her hair was stringy. She had a dish towel in her hand, and she spoke in a flat tone. "I'll fix your supper. It'll take a few minutes."

"Anything's all right," Jeff said. "Don't make any extra work for yourself, Mrs. Scroggins. While I'm waiting, I'll have a drink."

There was a bar at the side. He stepped that way

9

and poured a drink from the bottle standing there, then took a seat at the long table. He was weary from the long pull up through the mountains, but it was a good weariness. Another ride and he would be home.

Scroggins' son came in. He was about thirteen, thin, rangy and with a pimply face. His hair, long and messy, gave him a wild look. He apparently had noticed Jeff's horse, because he asked, "Want me to take care of your horse, mister? Want me to unsaddle him?"

"No, don't unsaddle him—I'm riding on," Jeff replied. "But you can feed him. Give him a short ration of oats."

"Sure will, mister," the boy said, turning to the door.

Scroggins came forward. "Been away, haven't you?"

"Yes. I took a trip."

"Just getting back?"

"That's right. How are things at the Park?"

"Just dandy," Scroggins said. "Yep, just dandy. Maybe I better see about your supper. Mom's forgetful."

He switched directions, angling toward the kitchen. Jeff sampled his drink. The blackjack game had apparently been suspended, but the two strangers were still at the small table. The young one had scooped up the cards and started a game of solitaire, and the older man was watching.

In a few minutes the woman brought in his supper. It wasn't first-rate but it was hot, and Jeff was hungry. As he worked on it he noticed Scroggins busy at the bar, but he paid little attention to him. Scroggins, he had heard, was a man who couldn't be trusted, but that didn't trouble him tonight. Soon, now, he would be gone.

One of the other men, however, the middle-aged one, left before he did. He got abruptly to his feet and started to the door, saying, "Gotta get ridin'. See you some day, Scroggins."

"Sure. See you again," Scroggins said.

The man left the room. Scroggins kept busy at the bar, and the man at the small table studied his cards. Jeff continued eating, then finished, pushed back his plate and stood up. He asked, "How much, Scroggins?"

"Dollar and a half, including everything," Scroggins said.

Jeff put the money on the table. He started for the door, but before he could reach it the man at the small table spoke.

"Hey, mister. You in a hurry?"

Jeff stopped, then looked at the man. "Why?"

"Did you know the man who was here when you came in? The one who left?"

"No."

"He knew you. He stiffened up the minute he saw you. Twice while you were eating, he touched your gun. Then he said he was leaving, but I haven't heard a horse. Could be he's still outside."

Jeff stood staring at the man. Who was he? What did he mean? He glanced at Scroggins, who stood motionless, looking shocked—or frightened.

"Scroggins," he said sharply. "What's this all about?"

The station agent shook his head. "I don't know what you mean, Jeff."

"Who was the man who left here?"

"Don't know. Honest."

The solitaire player smiled. He said, "Scroggins, you're a liar."

"But I—"

Jeff turned again to the man at the small table. "What's your name?"

"Brick Rawson. What do they call you?"

"Jeff Carmody."

The man put his cards aside. "I'm on the way to the Park. Meant to stay here for the night, but since what's happened I don't think I'd be comfortable. Like to have company?"

"Why not?"

Brick grinned. He stood up and checked his gun, then said, "How do you want to leave? By the front door, or the back?"

"It might be safest by the back."

"And what about Scroggins? He's the kind who—"

The stage agent reached under the bar, but before he could bring his rifle in sight, Brick flipped up his holster gun. Jeff had never seen anything faster. He hadn't even seen the motion of the man's arm, but there in his hand was his holster gun, covering Scroggins.

"Drop your rifle," Brick ordered. "Turn around and face the wall."

Scroggins didn't argue the matter. He dropped the rifle and turned to face the wall, and Brick stepped up to the bar. He leaned over and swung the barrel of his gun against the agent's head. Scroggins sank instantly to the floor.

"Now we'll take a look outside," Brick said.

He didn't seem at all excited. He looked calm, unperturbed, but the dispatch with which he had handled Scroggins was something to remember.

They went through the kitchen. Mrs. Scroggins had disappeared. Outside, for a moment, they stood in the deep shadows near the door. No one challenged their presence.

"You take one side, I'll take the other," Jeff whispered. "Circle to the front."

"Don't rush it, Jeff. Be seeing you."

Jeff circled half the building. His senses were sharply acute, but he still was bewildered by what was happening. Who was the man who had left the room? He had no idea; he was sure he hadn't known him. Then what was this all about? Why was someone after him, or was there any truth to what was going on?

A shot startled him, a shot followed by a hoarse cry, then two more shots. He started running instantly, hurrying around the front of the building. Someone was standing at the far corner. It was Brick Rawson. Almost at his feet lay a bulky, motionless figure.

"Found him crouching right where he is," Brick said flatly. "Gave him a chance to throw away his gun. He didn't."

Jeff stooped over the man and examined him briefly, then looked up. "He's dead, Brick."

"What did you expect?"

Jeff struck a match. He stared at the dead man's face, but it was wholly unfamiliar. He felt in the man's pockets but found nothing to tell who he was.

"I'll get my horse," Brick said.

Jeff stood up. He wasn't quite sure what they should do now. Perhaps they should remain here until word could be sent to the sheriff in Indian Bluff, but he doubted that that was what Brick meant to do.

"I'll go in and see Scroggins," Jeff said slowly. "He can send a report to the sheriff."

Brick shrugged indifferently. "Suit yourself, Jeff."

They climbed toward the pass under a moon-bright sky. Jeff led the way, taking advantage of the short cuts he knew, and, half an hour above Armand's Fork and after a sharp climb, they stopped to rest their horses. This was their first good chance to talk, a moment to which he had been looking forward. Brick Rawson interested him.

"This mountain country looks good," Brick said, lighting a cigarette. "But it's hard to believe you could find a place flat enough to run cattle."

"Wait until we drop over the pass," Jeff answered. "Eden Park is a tableland, wide and deep, well watered and with the best grass you ever saw."

"But how do you get cattle in and out?"

"Down the other side. It's an easy drive to Caldwell, at the rail head."

"Town in the Park, isn't there?"

"A place called Crestline."

"How many ranches?"

"Half a dozen, fair-sized. Several that are smaller. Not looking for a job, are you?"

"I think I've got one."

"Where?"

"Had a letter from an old friend. Matt Doberman. Maybe you know him."

"Yes, I know him," Jeff said slowly.

His eyes narrowed thoughtfully. Matt Doberman worked for Jeff's father on the Rocking H. But he had been just a rider. He hadn't been in position to hire anyone. But then, in the letter, he might not have offered Brick a job. His letter might have suggested that Grandy needed more workers. That was quite possible.

Brick studied his cigarette. He said, "Jeff, I don't ordinarily butt into something that isn't my concern."

"This time, I'm glad."

"You're sure you didn't know the man I shot?"

"No."

"Got any enemies?"

"A few, I suppose. Most men do. But this one I can't figure."

"Then think again," Brick said. "The man I shot was crouching at the corner, his gun out. He was waiting for you. It wasn't any accident. Where do you work in the Park?"

"For Grandy Holt."

Brick looked surprised. "The devil you say. Then you work for Doberman."

"Nope. For Grandy. My father."

"You said your name was Carmody."

"It is," Jeff said quietly. "My mother was a widow, and I was only three years old when she married Grandy Holt. Since then, he raised me. I've always called him father."

The expression on Brick's face was hard to read. He shook his head and laughed, but he didn't seem amused. And his eyes had hardened.

"We're going the same place, aren't we?" Jeff asked.

"Yes. The same place. Doberman wrote me there was another son. But he was away."

"I've come back."

"That could be awkward."

They sat facing each other, neither one smiling now. What was ahead, Jeff didn't know. He remembered the way Brick had whipped up his gun in the stage station, and he recalled what had happened in the darkness outside. A man had been killed. Ordinarily, a man felt it when he shot someone, but not this man. Brick had shown no emotion at all. This had obviously not been his first killing. He was a man to watch.

"How well do you know Doberman?" Brick asked suddenly.

"Not well," Jeff answered.

"Like him?"

"No."

A wry smile crossed Brick's face. "You've tagged him, anyhow. He's not very likeable. What are we going to do when we get to the Park?"

Jeff shrugged. "Who knows?"

"Suppose we find out."

"Suits me."

"Then we'll ride on."

They had rested their horses long enough. Jeff wheeled away, leading the way again, his shirt suddenly sticky with perspiration. As easily as he had suggested that they ride on, he could have reached for his gun. What might have happened then he didn't know. He could handle his gun quite well. Grandy had drilled him with it from the days of his childhood, but for every fast gun there was always one that was faster. He might have been able to match Brick Rawson, but he wasn't at all anxious to make the test.

Another thing worried him, too. Brick was an outsider, but in spite of that he seemed wholly confident. Why? What had happened in the Park during the past three months? What would he find at the Rocking H? His uneasiness deepened with every mile.

CHAPTER 2

They made it to the crest of the pass an hour after midnight, and there Jeff waved his arm in a half circle to the south. "Take a good look, Brick. Just below us is Eden Park."

"How wide?" Brick asked.

"A day's ride across it in almost any direction. It's broken here and there by timber, but where the land is clear it's the best meadow land in the country."

At night, and even with a fair light from the sky, it was impossible to get a good look at the Park, but he knew it so well he could fill in the details from his memory. Far off to the east, which was only a blur, was the Gitterhaul ranch, separated from Dan Hotchkiss' land by a dividing creek lined with straggling trees. Nearer was Risling's, and in a direct line to the south was the town of Crestline. To the west was Waldron's. Farther south was the Rocking H, and below it was the Zeigler ranch.

Jeff pointed out each one, knowing it wouldn't make much sense to Brick Rawson. But he was only talking anyhow, making conversation, sticking to a safe subject. They had made a number of other stops on their climb to the crest, but they hadn't been comfortable. Each man seemed frankly unsure of the other.

"Do we go through town on the way to the Rocking H?" Brick asked bluntly.

"No, we cut west and south above town. It saves time."

"When'll we get there?"

"Ought to make it by dawn."

"That far?"

"It's still quite a ride."

Brick lit another cigarette. "Who's the sheriff in Crestline?"

"Art McEllis."

"Honest?"

"Near as I know. He doesn't like me, but that's a personal matter."

Brick shifted in his saddle, then leaned forward. "Jeff, aren't you curious about me?"

"Sure."

"Then why haven't you questioned me?"

"Would it have done any good?"

"Nope."

"That's what I figured, Brick."

The man laughed softly. He said, "Jeff, I wish we were on the same side. 'Fraid it won't work out that way. Too damned bad."

Jeff managed a grin. "Ready to ride?"

"Any time you are."

They rode on, dropping down toward the Park. Two hours later they were slanting across what

Grandy sometimes called the roof of the world, his own name for the Park. He had been one of the first men to settle here.

Jeff couldn't remember his own father. He had been an Army man who had been killed in the Territory in an Apache raid. That was before Jeff had been a year old. Just before her death several years ago, his mother had given him a tintype picture of his father. It showed a slender, very erect young man in a uniform, his face thin, mustached and quite stern. "But it's not a good picture of him," his mother had said. "He laughed a great deal. He was kind and gentle. Don't think of him as a soldier. Think of him as a man who was good."

She had married Grandy Holt two years later, and so far as Jeff knew she never had regretted it. She had given Grandy two children—a son, Wade, now nineteen, and a daughter, Syl, a year younger. And during her lifetime she hadn't shown any favoritism. Nor had her husband. Grandy showed him the same consideration as his own children.

As Wade and Syl grew older, however, he had sensed a difference between him and them. Grandy was their father, not his. He had had a different father. This set him apart from them. He wasn't quite as good as they were. And, in a thousand little ways, they had showed it.

Actually, this hadn't worried him too much. He

had made up for their attitude by keeping busy. He was older, anyhow, and could do things they couldn't. Then, when he was old enough to ride out where he wanted, he had found companionship with Ferd and Vicki Waldron. This had separated him even more from Wade and Syl, and eventually he didn't feel close to them at all. They became strangers. He shared the same house with them and ate at the same table, over which Grandy presided. He was a part of the family group, but he felt kinship only with Grandy. And that was rather strange, because Wade and Syl were his half brother and half sister by blood, and Grandy his relative only by marriage.

He was thinking of them as he and Brick Rawson slanted across the Park toward the Rocking H. Grandy he didn't worry about. He and Grandy understood each other. Long ago they had set up a pattern of honesty with each other. If they disagreed, they said so. They talked it out. Sometimes they got excited, but they always knew where they stood. With Wade and Syl, it was different.

At nineteen, Wade was tall, slender and too damned attractive. Erratic, restless and impulsive, he drank too much and showed poor judgment in women. He liked to gamble but wasn't good at it, and he hated to lose; thus he could very easily get in trouble. He wore a gun, of course, since it made him feel like a man, but he didn't use it with skill. Grandy had tried to make him practice when he was younger, but he hadn't kept at it. These days he practiced, but he never would have the smoothness a man needed to be proficient.

And Syl—what was Syl like? That was a question he couldn't answer. She was beautiful—and as restless as Wade. She could ride and rope like a man, but she didn't like men. Jeff knew half a dozen men who had tried to get her interested in them without success. She seemed to avoid them. What was wrong with her, anyhow? Even Grandy was puzzled about her, and had talked to him about her. He had told Grandy not to worry, that Syl would work out all right—but he wasn't at all sure of it.

"Shouldn't we be getting there?" Brick asked.

The sky had turned light. Right now, in all probability, the cook at the Rocking H was up and was building his morning fires. They would make it in time for breakfast. He nodded. "Yep. Only a few miles."

Brick checked his gun, then said, his voice mocking, "Just a habit. Something I always do."

"Habit of mine, too," Jeff said deliberately.

He checked his own gun, then eased it into its holster, and they rode on together.

"That it?" Brick asked a few minutes later.

"Yep. That's it," Jeff said.

Ahead of them now, across a wide meadow,

they could see a cluster of ranch buildings. A high-roofed barn dominated the scene, but the main house, too, was quite large. Beyond it, and to the west, was a cabin and the bunkhouse. The corral and several sheds were south of the house, mostly out of sight.

"A big place, huh?" Brick said, sounding pleased.

"Big as we need," Jeff said.

They continued across the meadow. Jeff was wearing a studied smile, wanting to seem at ease, glad to get home. His muscles had tightened up, however, and he had a funny feeling in his stomach. Faint and far off he heard the breakfast gong.

"Gonna make it in time," Brick said.

No one was in sight as they rode into the yard, but someone must have heard them, because Matt Doberman came outside as they were dismounting and, tying their horses. Then he looked inside quickly and said something, and, as they turned toward the house, several others joined Doberman on the low porch. One was his brother, Wade, and one was old Andy Culp, but the others were strangers, men he didn't know. He noticed two in particular. One was thin, stooped and very dark-complexioned, and had a twisted body, with one shoulder several inches lower than the other. The second man was huge, thick-bodied and tall, with ruddy cheeks, sun-blistered lips and a flat nose. He was grinning.

"A welcoming committee, huh?" Brick said slyly.

Jeff took a quick look at him. A half-amused expression was on his face, and his eyes were twinkling. He didn't seem at all worried.

"Just some of the fellows," Jeff said.

"That so?"

On the porch, Wade and Doberman had had a brief conference. They now stood watching. Matt Doberman, heavy and wide-shouldered, was wearing his usual scowl. He had a deep-lined face, hard eyes and square, bulging jaws. He looked angry, but then he always looked angry. His expression was the same as it had been on the day Jeff hired him. He very nearly had decided not to take him on, but at the time they had needed another man desperately, and no one else had been available. Wade, too, was scowling, but, just as with Doberman, it didn't necessarily mean a thing. Whenever he was crossed, or when things didn't go right, or when he felt he had been slighted, Wade showed it in his face. He was extremely sensitive, a hard man to live with.

"Hello, Wade," Jeff said easily. "Where's Grandy?"

Wade didn't answer him. He leaned forward, and his words came out too high. "Why did you come home?"

"Now that's a funny question," Jeff said.

"I mean, we heard you got in trouble."

"If I did, I got out of it," Jeff said. "Where's Grandy?"

Wade looked uneasily at Doberman, who edged ahead and said, "Jeff, I'm sorry, but Grandy ain't been so good. In fact, he's a mighty sick man."

"Sick!" Jeff cried. "What's wrong with him?"

"A bum ticker. He's got to take it easy."

"Where is he? In his room?"

"Sure—but you can't see him."

"I what!"

"You can't see him, Jeff. The doc says he can't take any excitement. If you walked in on him, you might kill him."

Jeff felt he had been stunned. He couldn't believe what he had heard. Grandy wasn't an old man. He still was in his fifties, husky, tireless. He could ride with any man of thirty, could stick in the saddle from dawn to dusk and then sit in a poker game half the night and show no weariness. It was unthinkable that he was seriously ill. And why couldn't he see him? Why would it excite him?

Wade was talking, explaining, but at the same time making an accusation. "It's all your fault, Jeff. Grandy got sick right after you left, and after his fight with you. The doc says you caused it. If you go in to see him again—"

Jeff spoke sharply. "What do you know about my fight with Grandy?"

26

"I was there—in the barn. I heard it."

"Then you heard the end. Sure we quarreled, but we got over it."

"Grandy threw you out."

"He did no such thing, Wade, and you know it."

Wade bit his lips. "I heard what I heard. It looked to me like—"

They weren't getting any place like this. Jeff stared at the men on the porch, and, definitely, old Andy Culp shook his head in warning. But in warning of what? What did he mean? He felt like busting ahead and making his way to Grandy's room, even if he had to fight his way—but, damn it, he couldn't if Grandy was seriously ill. With an effort he held his temper under control, and, fastening his eyes on Wade, he said, "Wade, Grandy's my father, almost as much as yours. I intend to see him. Don't try to stop me."

A tense moment followed, and Jeff didn't know what was going to happen next. Then Doberman surprised him. "Now don't get all riled up, Jeff," the man said, grumbling. "You'll get to see Grandy. I reckon you've got the right. 'Course he ain't up so early as this. Why don't you come in and have breakfast?"

Brick spoke up quickly. "How about me?"

"And who the hell are you?" Doberman asked.

"My name's Brick Rawson. I'm looking for work. Met Jeff on the road. He said I might get a job here."

27

"I'll study about it," Doberman said. "We'll talk about it after breakfast."

It was Jeff's turn to be amused. Doberman had sent for Brick Rawson. Undoubtedly, the two were well acquainted but were acting like strangers.

"At least I'm welcome," Brick said under his breath.

"The day isn't over," Jeff said.

They trooped inside, and there was little talk while they ate. Wade sat defiantly at the head of the table, in Grandy's usual place. Doberman was at his right, the place that three months before had been Jeff's. Brick sat down across from Doberman, and Jeff took a seat down the table. He had hoped to get near Andy Culp, but two of the other men sandwiched him, and Jeff did not want to make issue of where he wanted to sit. Later on he would have a chance to see Andy. Wade again, too. And Doberman. His mind was flooded with questions.

He ate slowly, weighing what he could see. Grandy was ill, possibly incapacitated. That left Wade in charge, undoubtedly with Doberman to help him. Then what of the men around the table? All, excepting Andy, were strangers. The men he had expected to find here were gone—what did that mean? What had happened to the men who had been here? Where had the new ones come from? Some of the new ones might have drifted into the Park, but there was another possibility to be considered. Just as Doberman had sent for Brick, he might have sent for the others. And, if that was the case, what was the reason? What was Doberman planning?

Jeff had another cup of coffee. Syl wasn't here, but that, at least, wasn't strange. Syl never ate with the men. They had a private dining room in the house. Often, in the evening, the family ate there. And Syl always ate there or in the kitchen.

Wade finished his breakfast. He conferred with Doberman, then got to his feet. "I'll see if Grandy's awake," he said bluntly. "If he is, I'll see if he'll let you come in, Jeff."

"Thanks," Jeff said dryly.

He wasn't worried about Grandy's decision. They had quarreled the day he left, but they had patched it up. If he had left, however, at the height of their argument, Grandy still would have seen him. Grandy had never dodged an issue in his life. He met his problems head on.

Andy Culp left the room, but the others remained, and now, facing each other across the table, Doberman and Brick talked about a job. Jeff wondered for whose benefit it was being held—the other men at the table, or himself? In rapid-fire order, Doberman asked the proper questions of a prospective rider. Brick gave the correct answers, and was hired—on trial. Soon, undoubtedly, they would have a private conference.

Syl appeared suddenly in the door to the other part of the house. At a guess, Wade had seen her and told her who was here. This morning she was wearing boots, a brown divided skirt, a tan blouse and a neckerchief. Her hair was pinned tightly to her head, a fashion she affected when she planned to go riding. She was tall, slender and coldly beautiful. When she smiled she was dazzling, but she wasn't smiling now. Her lips had tightened, and her eyes looked hard.

Jeff stood up. "Good morning, Syl."

Her words were blunt. "Why did you come home?"

"Why not?"

"We heard you killed a man in Denver—that you were to be hung."

Jeff grinned. "Must have been a mistake."

"Grandy heard the same story. It almost killed him. Then you had to come home. We don't want you."

She was making a public announcement. When her father had been the head of the family, the policy had been to keep their quarrels a private matter. But maybe that didn't count any more. Or perhaps this meant that, when one member of the family had been thrown out of the group, the old rules went by the board.

Jeff glanced at the others at the table, but without thinking about them. He was struggling to understand Syl. He had never been close to her, it was true, but her bitterness this morning was unreasonable. It didn't fit her character. In the past she had been cruel to him, but never vicious. And most of that had been long ago. For the last year or so she had been rather friendly. She had been worried once about Wade, and had talked to him, openly seeking his help. Then why the change? What had happened to her? Apparently she had heard a story about some trouble he had had, but could that have been the reason?

Brick looked up at her, a bold, impudent expression on his face. "Want me to chase him off, ma'am? I'm good at chasing men off."

Syl stared down at him. "Who are you?"

"Just hired on. My name's Brick Rawson. Maybe I spoke out of turn, but I've been doing it all my life."

"Then you spoke out of turn again," Syl said sharply.

Wade reappeared, coming up behind his sister. He put his arm around her shoulders and looked past her at Jeff. "Grandy will see you again," he reported. "But you can stay for only a minute. And don't start anything. If you do, I'll break you in pieces."

The threat was ridiculous; it had a hollow sound, and Jeff made no answer. The important thing was that he was going to see Grandy. Turning from the table, he walked toward them.

CHAPTER 3

Wade led the way, Syl walking with him and Jeff following them. Someone was trailing him from the mess hall, but he didn't look back to see who it was. They went through the kitchen and parlor, and from there turned down the west wing corridor. He passed the door to his room. It was closed, and probably wasn't being used now. Across from it was a guest room, next was Syl's room and opposite that Wade's. Grandy's was at the end of the corridor.

It was a large room, more than a bedroom. It contained a fireplace, a desk, shelves of books and several comfortable chairs. His mother's sewing machine was still there. After the west wing had been built, one of the old bedrooms had been converted into a sewing room. But she had seldom used it. In the evenings, his mother had often spent her time here, doing her sewing while Grandy worked on his ledgers and records.

The big double bed was over at the side, and near it was a wide window opening on the yard and in view of the corral. This window was curtained now, as were the other windows, and when Jeff stepped inside the room there wasn't much light. He could make out the outline of a lumpy figure under the blankets on the bed, and he noticed a table near the head of the bed. On it was a pitcher of water and a glass, several bottles of medicine and several books. Grandy had always been a great person for reading. Many times in the past he had complained he never could find the time to keep up on his reading. Maybe now he was getting the chance he had wanted.

Wade and Syl had preceded him to the bed, and now Wade was talking in a hushed voice. "He's here, Grandy. Now, remember what the doctor said. No excitement."

"Bring him over," Grandy said.

His words were weak and the tone querulous. It didn't sound natural. Jeff stepped forward, and as he approached Wade and Syl made room for him. What he saw, then, shocked him. He had expected to find Grandy ill, but he hadn't thought he would look like this. Terribly thin, no color in his face, his eyes buried deep in his skull, his cheeks sunken in. He was scarcely recognizable.

"Hello, Grandy," Jeff said slowly, adding, "I didn't know you had been ill. If I had heard—"

Grandy moistened his lips. "Get out!"

Jeff stared wide-eyed at the man in the bed. He couldn't credit what he had heard. This wasn't Grandy who had told him to get out. Of course it was, but it didn't make sense. What had happened between them? What was wrong?

He started to speak again. "Grandy—"

But the man in the bed interrupted him again, his voice stronger. "Get out. I never want to see your face again. You are no son of mine. Get out!"

"But why, Grandy?"

The old man turned his head, as though appealing to Wade. "Throw him out. You've got the men to do it. Get him out of my sight. Tell everyone this. Say that Jeff Carmody is no son of mine, that I disown him. Say that to me Jeff Carmody is dead."

Jeff just stood there, motionless. He didn't say a word. He couldn't. This was like a sentence from a judge, but many times worse. He couldn't understand it, but he had heard it and couldn't deny it. Grandy had turned against him, was through with him, never wanted to see him again. The past was erased. His mother had been Grandy's wife, but he was nothing.

Wade took his arm, and from the other side came Matt Doberman, the person who had followed them here. Doberman spoke. "Outside, Jeff. You heard him."

"Yes. I heard him," Jeff said numbly.

He glanced at Wade and saw the triumphant look in the boy's eyes, sensed the excitement that had gripped him. Wade's expression said that here was a vindication of his rightful position. He, was the son of Grandy Holt—the only son. Jeff Carmody was finished.

"Outside," Doberman said again.

Jeff nodded, and as he turned he noticed Syl. There was a curious expression on her face. She seemed startled, almost frightened, but perhaps she was worried about Grandy. She had been looking at him, but now she was staring at her father, and as Jeff left she stooped over the bed. Then she said something to Grandy, but her words were too low to be heard.

They walked back to the parlor, and there they stopped. Jeff still felt dazed. His mind didn't seem to be working. He looked vaguely around the room.

"I guess you'll be riding on," Doberman said.

"You're damned right he'll be riding," Wade said. "We've got no place for him here."

Jeff stirred. "Yes, I'll be riding. But I don't know why Grandy feels the way he does. If he wasn't so sick, we could talk it out."

"Wouldn't make no difference," Doberman said. "The day you left, Grandy told me he was finished with you."

That was a direct lie. Jeff was sure of it, but it didn't seem worthwhile to argue about it. He said vaguely, "I suppose you're running the ranch, Doberman?"

"No—I am," Wade said hurriedly. "I've run the ranch since Grandy got sick. Doberman's top hand."

Jeff glanced from one to the other. Wade had been quick to assert his importance, and Doberman didn't question it. The truth, however, wasn't hard to see. Wade didn't have the qualities of leadership. He might think he was running the ranch, but actually it was Doberman who was in the saddle. Then, what was his game? What was he after? Jeff puzzled about this for a moment, then shrugged and turned away. It wasn't his problem any more. He had been disowned by the man who had been his father. He could saddle and ride.

"Where will you be going?" Doberman asked bluntly.

"Haven't decided," Jeff replied. "Don't know what I'll be doing."

Wade spoke, in his words a studied insult. "Do you need money?"

"No, I don't need money," Jeff said.

He walked to the door opening on the yard. Outside, he glanced from side to side. Most of the men he had seen at breakfast were standing around, two at the corral, two at the barn, two at the corner of the house, one near the cabin. By this time, most of them should have been away on the job. Or maybe that's where they were—on the job, deliberately stationed to cover the yard. Jeff considered the possibility for a moment, then shrugged, stepped into the yard and slanted toward the corral. If he was in danger, he couldn't do anything about it.

The two men at the corral were Brick and Andy
Culp. Brick was leaning against one of the posts,
and Andy was moving through the gate to catch a
horse. He was the only one doing anything. If
anything was planned, certainly Andy wasn't in
on it. And, probably, nothing had been planned.
Maybe, in placing the men where they were,
Doberman was merely playing safe.

Brick wore his impudent grin. Tall, slender,
self-assured, amused at what had happened. "So
you're leaving, huh?" he said. "Too bad."

"There'll be another day," Jeff said.

"And what does that mean?"

"Figure it out for yourself."

"Leaving the Park?"

"Why should I?"

"You might live longer."

Jeff managed a grin. "So I should be worried,
huh?"

"Can't you read the signs?"

"Nope. They're all mixed up," Jeff said slowly.
"But I'll study them, Brick. Maybe I'll come up
with something."

Andy Culp had roped a horse and brought it
outside. In lifting the saddle he slipped and fell to
the ground. He sat up and started swearing. He
wasn't hurt. He was angry, furiously angry, and
his words were colorful. Brick started laughing,
and even Jeff had to smile. He stepped toward
Andy, picked up the saddle and put it on the horse.

"You might give me a hand, too," Andy snarled. "I was the one who got dumped."

"You're not that old," Jeff said.

He stooped over, however, and helped Andy to his feet. As he did, Andy spoke again, his words barely a whisper. "See me in town." And an instant later, jerking away, he glared at his horse and started swearing again.

Jeff stepped back, laughing and slapping his leg. He glanced at Brick, wondering whether he had caught the whispered message. If he had, however, his face didn't show it. "There's one on every ranch," he said, laughing.

"Yep, on every ranch," Jeff agreed.

Andy Culp, in his seventies now, was stooped, and his deeply wrinkled skin was like leather, his eyes watery. He should have retired years before, but he wouldn't think of it. "I've lived in the saddle all my life," he often said. "That's the way I'll die." He really meant it.

Jeff untied his horse. He swung into the saddle and then glanced back through the yard. Wade, Syl and Doberman had come outside and were watching. The others, still around the yard, were watching, too. And maybe from inside Grandy was watching. Jeff's expression turned stony. He raised his arm and waved, but no one waved back.

"Take my advice," Brick said. "Keep riding."

"I'll think about it," Jeff said.

He wheeled away, turning in the direction of Crestline, and, until he was out of sight of the ranch, didn't look back.

Matt Doberman was just under forty. He had had a varied career, most of it in conflict with the law but not in a way to attract attention. He had ridden with King Fisher, Beaudry, the Carson brothers and the Llano Turner band. He had been one of the crowd, unnamed, unlisted. He had made his cut on every job he had worked, but the total amount each year didn't amount to much more than a wage. And at times, to make ends meet, he had taken legitimate work. For years he had dreamed of the big job he would pull off someday, but until he came to Eden Park he didn't know what it would be.

Even then, at the beginning, he didn't see it. When he came to Eden Park he had been drifting, looking for a job that would keep him running until he could make a new connection. Then, by chance, two things happened. Jeff Carmody went away on a trip, and Grandy got sick. This left Wade as the theoretical head of the ranch, and Wade could be handled. There were a few others among the men who might have taken his place, but he could act tough and aggressive, and a little bluff helped along. Inside of a week of Grandy's illness, Doberman was running things.

For a time, then, Doberman worried that Jeff

might get back, but as time went on he didn't, and gradually the men who had been here were replaced. His own plans changed, too. In the beginning he had thought only of stripping the range and Grandy's bank account. But what he was planning now was something much larger. And it was sound, too. A beautiful thing to look at.

He himself had changed in the last three months. He had grown in stature. He could sense the difference in his makeup. He had moved up through the ranks, become a person of importance. A leader. No longer was he one of the crowd. He had proved it, definitely, when he ran into Vegas and John Creel in town. He hadn't sent for them. They had been on a mission of their own, but he knew them, talked to them and hired them. Today they took his orders. A year ago they wouldn't have.

Lanier, Bealer, Fiske, Murphey and the others he had sent for. They had been members of the crowd, and they were now. But today they were members of *his* crowd. He was the chief. Undisputed. It was good to feel that way. And it had been easy—that was the amazing thing. Years ago, he could have been where he was now. But what of it? He was there now, and he would stay there.

Doberman watched Jeff out of sight, then turned and said what he thought was wise. "Too bad. I always liked Jeff Carmody. Wonder what'll happen to him?"

"I don't give a damn," Wade said bluntly.

Syl was frowning. "Wade, you don't mean it."

"Sure I do."

"I don't feel that way," Syl said. "I'm sorry for him."

Doberman felt like laughing. Instead, he made his voice gruff. "You better get the men to work, Wade. We talked earlier about what had to be done. You start 'em. I'll join you later. I want to have a longer talk with the new man, Brick Rawson."

"Just leave it to me," Wade said.

Doberman signaled to Brick, then walked to the cabin. He was pacing the floor when Brick came in, and he grinned and said, "Howdy, Brick. Glad you could come."

"Wasn't busy," Brick said. "You've got quite a crowd."

"Know some of them, huh?"

"Most of them. What are you doing? Starting a war?"

Doberman laughed. "Nope. I don't think it'll come to that, but I'm playing it safe. What do you think of Syl?"

"Nice."

"Is that all you can say?"

"Nope, I could say more," Brick admitted. "Is she my job?"

"That's part of the plan. Like it?"

"Might be interesting."

"Then get to work. Maybe I can help, but we'll talk about her later. First I want to know something else. How come you got here with Jeff Carmody?"

"Just happened," Brick said easily.

Doberman stared at the man. He had been shocked when he saw Jeff, and seeing him with Brick had rattled him. He wished suddenly that he knew Brick better. Actually, he knew very little about him. They had ridden together for several months under Llano, and when their crowd broke up he remembered where Brick had been going. He knew Brick was good with his gun, that he was reckless, afraid of nothing and personally attractive. He knew he had been loyal to Llano, but beyond that not much more.

"Damn it, Brick," he said suddenly. "This fellow Jeff Carmody could cause us a lot of trouble. You could have saved us that if you'd dropped him last night."

"You mean I should have shot him?"

"Why not?"

"And why should I? How did I know Jeff Carmody was Grandy Holt's son? Their names are different. In your letter you said nothing of anyone named Carmody."

"Did you come over the pass?"

"Yes."

42

"I had a man over the pass, watching for Jeff Carmody. A man at Armand's Fork. His name was Soapy Wibel."

"He's dead."

Doberman took a deep breath. "How did that happen?"

"He rubbed me the wrong way, Doberman. And don't jump me. I didn't know who he was or why he was there. And if you don't like it, to hell with you."

They stood facing each other, momentarily silent. Doberman couldn't figure what Brick was thinking. It was true he had said nothing of stationing a man at Armand's Fork. It probably was true that Brick hadn't known the man. He could have been totally unaware of Wibel's connection here. But Doberman still didn't like what had happened. And he didn't like the way Brick had arrived here, riding with Jeff.

"Weigh it up yourself, Doberman," Brick was saying. "I can stay here or I can ride. It's up to you. I don't need your job."

"And I don't need you," Doberman snapped back. "I don't need you, but I could use you. It would be worthwhile, too. You decide. Throw in with us—or ride. Which will it be?"

Brick turned to the window. Doberman, looking past him, could see Syl in the yard, and before Brick swung around Doberman knew what his answer would be.

CHAPTER 4

Several miles up the road Jeff swung north. After a time he came to the Eden River, the northern border of the Rocking H. There, under the trees, he stopped briefly.

He had hit the river at a point he knew quite well. At some places the Eden was wide and shallow, but along this part was a series of deep pools. This was where he had learned to swim, where he had learned to fish. There were a number of big, brown speckled trout in the river, but landing one wasn't easy. Grandy had taught him how to go about it. "Drop your line in the riffle above the pool," Grandy had said. "Then float it down above the big ones. When one hits, don't jerk it out of his mouth. Let him have it. Make sure he's on your line before you go after him." He had had several good strikes before he developed the patience to let the trout take the bait.

Those days when he was growing up had been good days, days of learning new things. When they came up here they would go fishing, then take a dip in one of the pools, and afterwards there was always time for a practice session with his gun. Grandy had started him with a holster gun when he was only eight, and the kick of it when he fired it had soon made his arm sore. His mother hadn't approved his learning to use a gun, but Grandy had insisted on it. "I don't want him to ever have to use it on another man," Grandy said soberly, "but, if it works out that he has to, I want him to be ready."

Jeff whipped his hand to his holster, snapping up his gun. He put it away again, wondering what Brick would think if he could see it. If the man asked about him, Wade might report he was pretty good with his gun, but even Wade didn't know how fast he was. He had built up no reputation. Fortunately, he hadn't had to.

He crossed the river, and now, above the Eden, he was on Abe Waldron's land. From here it wasn't more than half an hour to the Waldron ranch. He headed in that direction.

It wasn't by accident or chance that he had turned this way. No matter what might have happened at home, his next trip would have been here, although he wasn't sure what kind of reception he would get. In the old days, however, he would have been welcomed. In the old days . . .

How many times had he been here in the past? It was impossible to count the number. From the days of his childhood, the Waldron ranch had been a second home. In the beginning, Ferd had been the attraction. They had been the same age and had become inseparable companions, and Ferd's sister Vicki, several years younger, had

45

often trailed along with them. He had enjoyed their company more than he had Wade's and Syl's. Ferd and Vicki took him on his own value. He was no interloper. He belonged.

They had had wonderful times together, and as the years passed a rather strange thing had happened. Or perhaps it wasn't strange. Perhaps it had been a natural thing to look at Vicki and discover that he really enjoyed having her along—that she was exciting.

He always would remember the many trips to the Waldron ranch, but one above all others he would never forget. On that evening, only three months before, he had driven there by wagon, carrying Ferd's body home. Abe had been shocked when he heard what had happened, and his wife, Ruth, had gone to pieces. Vicki had fainted. But she had recovered quickly, and what she said afterwards had been bitter and harsh, and aimed straight at him. She had blamed him for Ferd's death, and in a way she had been right.

She had faced him, her cheeks drained of all color but her eyes blazing. "Why did you use Ferd? Why didn't you ride the horse yourself?"

"I tried to," he had explained. "The horse threw me. Then Ferd tried."

"But why did you let him? If you couldn't ride the horse, you knew Ferd couldn't have."

"No, Vicki. Ferd was a better wrangler than I.

Anyhow, it was an accident. Ferd hit one of the posts when he fell."

In her state of shock, however, Vicki couldn't see it that way. "It was an outlaw horse," she had said. "I heard you telling Ferd about it yesterday. You brought him over to your ranch. You encouraged him to ride the horse. You killed him as surely as though you had put a bullet through his heart."

After he got back home, he had shot the horse. That was what had brought on his quarrel with Grandy. And, actually, Grandy had been right in criticizing him for what he had done. In time, the horse could have been broken and used. Ferd's death hadn't been the horse's responsibility. What had happened had been an accident.

He hadn't seen the Waldron since. He had left the Park that night—just to get away for a while. Or maybe he had run away, run away from his restlessness—away from Vicki and her parents, and Ferd, now dead. But if he had run, he was back home again.

The Waldron ranch was ahead, now. As Jeff rode into the yard and tied his horse, he heard someone on the porch. Looking that way he saw Mrs. Waldron. She was a rather small but very energetic woman, whose hair was still dark. As he walked toward her, he noticed that she was smiling. If she was at all disturbed, she didn't show it.

"I'm glad you're back, Jeff," she said. "Abe is away. Vicki, too. Would you like to come in? I've coffee on the stove."

"Yes. I'd like to come in," Jeff said.

They sat at the table in the kitchen, and Mrs. Waldron first spoke of Grandy. "We've been worried about him. They say he's not at all well. He's not even supposed to have visitors. Have you seen him?"

"Yes, I've seen him," Jeff said. But he didn't want to talk about Grandy. He took a deep breath, then said steadily, "I'd like to know where Ferd's buried. I didn't come to the funeral. I—I had to get away for a while."

She seemed to understand. "I think I know how you felt, Jeff. Our son is buried in the grove above the house where you all three played as children. You can easily find the marker. And Jeff—I don't blame you for what happened. I know it was an accident. Abe feels that way, too."

"And Vicki?"

She was frowning now. "Vicki never mentions your name. I'm sure that in her heart she knows it was an accident, but she's very stubborn, very proud and very young. One of these days—"

They heard horses in the yard, and a moment later Abe and Vicki came in. They stopped just inside the door, and for a moment both were silent. Vicki stiffened instantly. Abe looked surprised, too, but he recovered quickly. He

48

stepped forward and put out his hand. "Hello, Jeff. I'm glad you're back." Then he looked uncertainly at his daughter.

"I'm not glad he's back," Vicki said sharply. "Maybe you've forgotten Ferd. I haven't."

Mrs. Waldron spoke slowly. "Ferd was our son, Vicki. We loved him."

"And you're entertaining the man who killed him."

"No, Vicki, you're wrong," Abe said. "What happened was an accident."

"I don't call it an accident," Vicki said, flaring up. "I know things about it that you don't know. I'll leave. When you get rid of the man who killed my brother, I'll come back."

She walked swiftly to the door and disappeared outside.

Mrs. Waldron broke the uncomfortable silence that followed, saying, "I'm sorry, Jeff, but I was afraid Vicki would be like this. I've tried to talk to her, but she won't listen. In time she'll change."

"She'll have to," Abe growled. "Bitterness is like poison. She's no longer the same girl."

Something Vicki had said stuck in Jeff's mind. He asked, "What did she mean by saying that she knew something you didn't?"

"I've no idea at all," Abe said. "Unless—"

"Unless what?"

"Vicki's been seeing a lot of Wade lately. I

don't think she likes him. I think she turned to him in defiance of you, but Wade could have said something."

Jeff considered that for a moment, but finally shook his head. Wade could have told her nothing about the accident that he hadn't already mentioned. He got up and walked to the door.

"You don't have to hurry off," Abe said. "Have you seen Grandy?"

"Briefly."

The thin, gaunt man scrubbed his jaw, looking worried. "I'm glad you're back. What I've seen at the Rocking H I haven't liked. Most of the old riders are gone. Doberman's brought in a new crew, some of them hard-looking characters. One is a giant called Lanier. Another, with a warped, crooked body, goes by the name of Vegas. And some of the others . . . At least, I'll feel better with you riding herd."

Jeff spoke bleakly. "I won't be riding herd."

"But why? I expected—"

"I told you I saw Grandy, and I did. It wasn't pleasant, and I don't understand it. I was told to get out."

"By Grandy!"

"Yes—by Grandy himself."

"I don't believe it."

"I can't either, but that's what happened. And I don't know what to do. I've been disowned. They say Grandy is dying, and maybe, since he married my mother, I should have certain rights. But I don't feel like fighting. I can get along. The only thing that bothers me is the way it happened. I thought a lot of Grandy."

"And he thought a lot of you," Abe said instantly. "He told me once that he felt you were as much his own son as though he had fathered you himself. He meant it, too, and it isn't likely he changed. What have they done to him since he got sick?"

"I don't know."

"What will you do?"

"I can't tell you that, Abe."

"You could stay here. I'll have a talk with Vicki. She needs a spanking, an old-fashioned spanking."

Jeff smiled but shook his head. The way Vicki felt, he couldn't stay here. He had been in love with her. To face her scorn and hatred, day in and day out, was too much to carry. "No, I'll ride on to Crestline," he decided aloud. "I'll figure things out in a few days."

He went outside. Vicki was standing in the scant shade of the barn, and when she saw him she straightened and stared at him defiantly. He hadn't noticed until right now that she was wearing a riding habit she had picked out particularly for him. She had bought it a month before Ferd's death. It was tan and fit close across her hips, and, without the jacket, it emphasized her narrow waist. The blouse was tight, too, revealing her deep bosom. She wasn't a tall girl, but that had never bothered him.

"Jeff, you don't have to hurry," Mrs. Waldron said from the door.

"I'll be by again," Jeff said.

He crossed to where he had tied his horse and swung into the saddle; then, ignoring Vicki, he circled the house and headed to the grove just beyond. There, under the trees where they had played as children, he found the marker where Ferd had been buried, a stone cairn surmounted by a cross. He dismounted near it, pulled off his hat and then stood silent. Memories flooded back, so vivid they hurt. His throat choked up, and tears filmed his eyes. In the years ahead he might make other friends, some close, but no one ever would take Ferd's place.

How long he stood there he didn't know, but finally, breaking the chains of the past, he remounted, then looked back at the house. Vicki was watching him from the corner, and behind her were her parents. As he rode away, they waved. Vicki didn't.

CHAPTER 5

The first settlers in the Park had had no town. In those days they had had to wagon in supplies from Caldwell, a long and boring trip. Eventually, however, a grocer in Caldwell had been persuaded to open a branch store in the Park. The following year, a stage line had agreed to make a weekly run for passengers, freight and mail. About this time, a cowhand who had done some forge work as a youngster set up shop near the store. A saloon had been next, and the day the saloon opened those in the Park realized they had a town, a gathering place, a center to ride to.

They had called it Crestline, and in the beginning it wasn't much of a town. It still wasn't, but it had grown with the years and was adequate to the needs of the Park. The area had been organized politically, and the town now had a courthouse, two new stores, a stage station, a barbershop, a restaurant, a bank and a harness and saddle shop. A school had been built, and across from it was a church. And, of course, there still was the smithy, the saloon, a corral and maybe a dozen dwellings. Nowadays, the stage line from Caldwell made four trips a week. A stage line also made it to Crestline from Indian Bluff, over the pass.

Jeff stuck to the road after leaving Abe Waldron's. He took his time, since he was beginning to feel the strain of his long ride. His muscles were sore, his eyes smarted and the bristle of his beard annoyed him. The hot sun beat down at his shoulders, sucking strength from his body.

It was a long pull to Crestline, but he made it late in the afternoon, pulling in at the corral, where his horse could be cared for. He swung to the ground, stiff, his legs sore and his back aching.

Will Shackle came out of the barn, recognized him and gasped. "Jeff! Is that really you. We thought—"

"You thought what?" Jeff asked.

Will grinned. "Nothing much, I guess. Heard about some trouble you had in Denver, but we must have been wrong. Glad you're back."

What was this story about trouble in Denver? Wade had mentioned it this morning, then Syl. He wondered who had started the rumor. It might be interesting to find out.

"Take care of my horse, Will," he ordered. "Rub him down well."

"When will you want him, Jeff?"

"I don't know. Not right away. He needs a rest."

"By God, I'm sure glad you're back," Will said again.

Will was quite old now, and he was partially

crippled. Because he drank too much and wasn't very dependable, he probably didn't rate very high in the Park, but his words were welcome.

How long he would feel that way, however, Jeff wasn't sure. Public sentiment was a tenuous thing. He had left Grandy to go on a vague trip, and he had stayed away when his help might have been needed. Then there were rumors of some trouble he had had in Denver. And now, before dark, people were going to hear that Grandy had disowned him. To many, that would seem very significant.

"I suppose you'll be running the Rocking H from now on," Will said.

Jeff felt suddenly irritated. "I just got back. I don't know what I'm going to do."

He jerked around and crossed the saddling yard, then glanced along the street. Half a dozen saddled horses were here and there at the tie rails, several in front of the saloon. Two men were on the porch of the Boston store, another was crossing from the courthouse to the bank. Down beyond the barbershop three boys were playing marbles, and nearer, on the porch of the sheriff's office, was his dog—a good sign that he was inside.

Jeff wanted to see the doctor for a firsthand report on Grandy's condition. Beyond that, he needed a shave, food and a place to stay. The matter of a place to stay might be a problem.

Crestline had no hotel. If a man had had too much to drink, Hap Ibberton sometimes put him up for the night in the saloon. Doc Hyman had extra rooms, too, but they were saved for those who needed his services. Mrs. Hoover occasionally took roomers, but because she was an incessant talker he didn't want to go there. A wry smile crossed his face. In all probability he would spend the night in the open, down by the river, but he knew he couldn't continue such an arrangement very long.

He started down the street, tentatively deciding to start with a shave, but several paces past the sheriff's office he heard someone calling his name and, looking back, saw McEllis had stepped outside.

"Noticed you through the window," McEllis said. "In a hurry, Jeff?"

"Nope. Not at all."

"Mind coming in for a minute?"

He shook his head, but without looking forward to the meeting. He and Art McEllis never had been comfortable with each other—why, he didn't know. He couldn't look in the past and point out any specific trouble that was responsible for their antagonism. But it was undeniably there. He had talked to Grandy about it one time, and Grandy had said he couldn't account for it, either. "You just rub each other the wrong way," he had guessed. "That happens, sometimes. I've known men I just didn't like, and for no reason. I just didn't like 'em."

McEllis was near forty. He had a solid body, heavy without being fat. He had powerful shoulders, sturdy legs and a thick neck. His face looked chubby, and he had thick, black hair and bushy eyebrows. He wore a clipped mustache over tight, thin lips, and he didn't smile easily. Or at least, he didn't smile for Jeff.

He followed the sheriff into the office. It was a small office, hot and stuffy even though the windows were open. The room contained a desk, several chairs, a safe, a file cabinet and a corner closet. On one side wall was a bulletin board, and on it were a number of wanted posters.

"You've been away, Jeff," the sheriff said. "Where?"

The talk very nearly ended right there, in an explosion. Where he had been was his own business; he didn't have to make a report. He almost said so, violently. But he held his temper, and when he spoke his words were casual. "Took a trip. That's all."

"Heard something about you being in Denver."

Jeff was silent for a moment. How did a man fight a rumor, a story from far away? He suddenly grinned. "Yep. I was in Denver."

"Heard you had some trouble."

"Killed six men. Held up two banks. No, I think it was three."

His answer didn't seem to strike the sheriff as funny at all. He said, with rising anger, "I don't like that kind of talk. I want the truth."

"Then maybe you better wire Denver and find out."

"I think I will."

"Go ahead, Sheriff. Anything else?"

"Yes. One other thing. If I need you, where can I find you? From what Wade told me a few minutes ago, you won't be staying at the Rocking H."

Jeff was a little surprised. Wade had lost very little time in spreading the news. But then, he should have expected that.

"Well, what are your plans?" the sheriff was asking.

He waved his arm vaguely. "Haven't any."

"Wade said you'd be leaving the Park."

"Might. Haven't decided."

"No other jobs to be had."

"Sheriff, there are always jobs."

"Not for you. Not since what Grandy said. Not for a man whose record isn't clean."

Jeff swung to the window to mask the anger that was gripping him. He wanted to tell the sheriff a few things. He wanted to whip around and go after him, but if he did he could easily end up in jail, and he couldn't afford that. Off and on throughout the morning and afternoon he had been puzzling over Andy Culp's whisper. *"See me in town.*" He had to meet him. He had to find out what Andy could tell him. It might be wholly unimportant, but on the other hand it might be something vital. Andy had been at the Rocking H for years. He was as much a part of the ranch as the buildings, and he had been close to Grandy. Before Jeff made any other decisions, he had to see Andy.

"We haven't had any trouble in the Park in years," McEllis said heavily. "I'm not going to stand for any, now."

"And what does that mean?" Jeff asked.

"It means this. I know, and everyone knows, that your mother married Grandy. In a way, some folks might think it gave you a claim on part of the Rocking H. But a father can disown his son. Don't get any ideas in your head that you can claim a part of Grandy's land. Don't start anything."

Jeff looked around. He managed a grin. "What are you doing, Sheriff? Borrowing trouble?"

"I just ain't gonna put up for any foolishness."

"Is that all?"

"Right now, yes. But don't forget what I said."

"Thanks," Jeff said dryly.

He wheeled away, stepped outside and moved on down the street. A spring wagon had just pulled into town. Ad Zeigler was driving it, and his wife was with him. The Zeigler ranch was south and west of Crestline. Jeff had been there many times, and he knew Ad and Maud Zeigler quite well. Ad was capable, energetic and a little headstrong, but they got along quite well. Maud, still pretty, was one of the best cooks in the Park, and she had invited Jeff for supper often in the past. Noticing them, Jeff waved, and Ad called a greeting. Maud, however, quickly looked the other way. She said something sharply to her husband and he answered her angrily, but Maud's back was board-stiff. What could be the reason for it? He could think of only one thing. To Maud, everything looked white or black. It must be that she had heard the story of what he had supposedly done in Denver. Damn it, that rumor was going to hurt him.

He walked on, past the bank and the harness shop, and in the barbershop he had a shave and a haircut. There, Pops Jelbert treated Jeff as casually as though he had never been away. As he worked he talked, covering a dozen different subjects. Pops caught all the gossip in the Park. He sifted it and passed it on to whoever would listen. Cora Risling was expecting a new baby, her fifth. The Gitterhaul boys had had the measles. Dan Hotchkiss had lost his two men. He needed someone badly but hadn't been able to find anyone. There had been a fire at the Zeiglers', but it hadn't been serious. Everyone was sure the market would improve before the fall drive to Caldwell.

"Ain't said much about the Rocking H," Pops said finally.

"Go ahead," Jeff said.

"They've throwed you out, but of course that ain't news. Wade struts around town, acting like he was running things. He doesn't. Doberman calls the turn. He's got good backing, too. A gunslinger named Vegas. Another named Creel."

Jeff climbed out of the chair. He said, "Tell me more about Wade."

"He's been gambling a lot."

"Losing?"

"He dropped more than a thousand last week. He's dipping heavy into Grandy's bank account."

"And what about me, Pops? What's this story about Denver?"

"I take it it ain't true."

Jeff laughed. "I don't know. Let's hear it first."

"They say you killed some man in Denver."

"And that's all?"

"Nope. A woman was involved. You were caught in her room by her husband."

"Who started the story?"

"It's hard to nail down a story like that. Heard it first, I think, from one of the men from the Rocking H, a man named Murphey. Ibberton got the story from Creel. I heard somewhere it was in the *Denver Post*. Don't know where that started."

If that story wasn't smashed, he might have

to live in its shadow for years. He had to do something right away, and he decided to use Pops Jelbert. He said, "Pops, I'd like to see that article in the newspaper, or any other proof that I shot some man in Denver. Suppose you pass out the news that I'll pay a thousand dollars for it. I've got the money in the bank."

"That ought to do it," Pops said. "I'll spread the news."

From the barbershop, Jeff went directly to the restaurant run by Ruth Sennett and her daughter Gwen. He was early for the evening meal, but when he came in Gwen said it was almost ready. She brought him a cup of coffee, then escaped from the kitchen to spend a few minutes at his table.

Gwen was tall and slender, with honey-colored hair and blue eyes. She said the freckles that splashed her face spoiled her appearance, but no one Jeff knew had ever objected to them. She was quite popular with everyone. There were a number of single men in the Park, and undoubtedly she had had a good many chances to get married. He often wondered why she had put it off.

Sitting across the table, Gwen cupped her chin in her hands and stared at him, frowning.

"What's wrong?" Jeff asked.

Gwen sighed. "What was she like—the woman in Denver? Was she very beautiful?"

"Very beautiful. She had two heads."

"So you ran away. But if I'd been the woman in Denver, you wouldn't have gotten away. Of course I don't believe the story at all. It's my hard luck that you're interested in only Vicki Waldron. If it hadn't been for her, I'd have trapped you long ago."

Jeff laughed, then said, "Gwen, you can do much better than me. When are you going to pick a man?"

"Do I have to?"

"Why not?"

She straightened and dropped her hands, then said, "Jeff, what do you think of Ben Adams?"

Ben worked for Ad Zeigler. He was steady, quiet and a damned good man around the place. Jeff would have liked to have him on the Rocking H. "I think it's a good choice," he said instantly.

"I didn't say I had made a choice," Gwen said. "I just—asked a question."

"Take him."

"Maybe—or maybe I'll be an old maid. Don't you think I'd be an attractive old maid?"

"Not at all."

Her mother interrupted them, calling Gwen to the kitchen, and Jeff relaxed at the table, rather pleased at what Gwen had said. Ben Adams wasn't a flashy person. He was tall and gaunt and not much on looks, but he did his job, saved his money and one of these days would have a place of his own.

Gwen brought his supper, and while he was eating several others came in, among them Dan Hotchkiss. Dan joined Jeff at the table and said, with characteristic directness, "Jeff, what's this about you quitting the Rocking H?"

"That's putting it in a nice way, Dan."

"Then it's true?"

"I'm afraid it is."

"Then how about you going to work for me? I can't pay you what you're worth, but I sure need help. Maybe we could work out some kind of deal."

Dan, short, stocky and about thirty, was an intense person who drove himself hard. He had a wife and three young children. Jeff knew his wife and liked her, and Dan was a man he could have worked with. Here, then, was a job in the Park he could take—if he wanted to stay. The question was what to do.

"Dan, I don't know how to answer you," he said slowly. "I need a chance to straighten out my thinking."

"Then do it on the job. Go to work for me on a day-by-day basis. Think about it."

"I couldn't ride tonight. My horse is tuckered out."

"You could borrow one from Will Shackle."

Ad Zeigler came in with his wife, and they took

64

a table not too far away. Ad spoke to him, but Maud didn't look in his direction.

Gwen brought Dan's meal, then a few minutes later stopped again at their table. "This will interest you, Jeff," she said soberly. "A man just came in and said there was an accident at the Rocking H. Andy Culp was killed, cleaning his gun."

An icy chill ran over Jeff's body. He half stood, then sank back in his chair. Andy was dead? An accident while cleaning his gun? He couldn't believe it. He shook his head numbly from side to side.

"That's terrible," Dan said. "Andy was a fine man. Careful of his gun. How could it have happened?"

Jeff didn't answer, but he felt an impulse to say that it hadn't been an accident, that it had been murder. But how could he prove a thing like that? With guns an accident was always possible. Or it could have been made to look like an accident. At any rate, Andy wouldn't be coming in to town to talk to him. Whatever message he had had wouldn't be delivered now.

"I'll see you outside, Dan—later," he said thickly.

Several Rocking H horses were at the tie rail in front of the saloon. Jeff pushed through the door. He wanted a direct report on how Andy had been killed. What it might lead to he didn't know, and at this point he didn't much care.

A dozen men were along the bar. He recognized several from having seen them at breakfast, but Wade wasn't among them, nor was Matt Doberman. With the group, however, was Brick Rawson, and Jeff called, "Brick, I want to see you for a minute."

The man looked around. He didn't seem at all troubled. "Hi, there, Jeff. Let me buy you a drink."

"We'll have it some other time. Let's go outside."

At the bar he noticed the twisted figure of the gunslinger, Vegas, and near him the giant Lanier. They and several others turned to follow Brick, who had shrugged and started for the door. Without much question, Brick was going to have all the re-enforcements he needed. That, however, was something to worry about later.

Jeff waited at the door for Brick, who was shaking his head. "You're just a plumb damned fool."

"Can't help it," Jeff said.

They went outside, turned up the street and stopped beyond the corner. In front of the saloon, Vegas, Lanier and the others stood watching, not sure what to expect. Across the street, McEllis came from his office.

Jeff paid no attention to the others in sight.

He said, "Brick, what happened to Andy Culp?"

"The old man? An accident."

"Who saw it?"

Brick pushed back his hat. A curious expression crossed his face. "You mean maybe it wasn't an accident?"

"That's what I'm wondering. Who saw it?"

"As I've heard it, no one. Who would have worried about him, anyhow?"

Jeff stared straight at him. "Back there at the corral, when I helped Andy up, he whispered he wanted to see me in town. If you heard him—"

"By God, I ought to—I don't go in for murder, Jeff. I didn't hear what the old man said—and to hell with you."

Brick had stiffened angrily, his face ruddy with color. Jeff had the feeling that he was telling the truth, that perhaps Brick had really had nothing to do with Andy's death. But that didn't alter the possibilities. He still wanted to know how the old man had died.

"You're asking for trouble," Brick said. "I can see what's coming. Use your head, man. As I heard it, Andy's death was an accident. Challenge it and Doberman will prove you're a liar. Then where will you stand?"

"You're in with a fine crowd," Jeff said caustically.

"Let me worry about that."

Jeff wondered what Brick was really like. He

didn't seem to fit in with men like Doberman and Vegas and the others now at the Rocking H. Or maybe he did. He shrugged and turned away.

"Where are you going, Jeff?" Brick called.

"I've found a job," he answered. "I'll be around, Brick. I told you I liked the Park."

Jeff slanted across the street. He had one other thing to do before he went to Will Shackle to borrow a horse. He wanted to see Doc Hyman. Fortunately the doctor was in.

"Expected you'd look me up," he said as he opened the door. "Come in. Have a chair."

"No, I can't stay," Jeff answered. "Tell me about Grandy."

"He's a sick man. A mighty sick man."

"You mean he won't live?"

"Jeff, how he's hung on this long I can't understand. He may slip away any day. It's hard to know what to expect. He's weak, and in constant pain, and there's not much I can do for him. I go out to see him twice a week, but frankly it's a waste of time. I wish I could say something else, but I've got to tell the truth."

"It was his heart?" Jeff asked.

"Yes. A block in the vein near the heart. We don't know what causes a thing like that. Sometimes it kills a man quickly, or it can take longer."

"Is there a chance for him at all?"

"I'll answer you this way. I had a patient like Grandy long ago. He lived three years—in bed. He lived that long only because of constant care."

Jeff shook his head. He knew Grandy. He wouldn't want to live if he had to spend his time in bed. It would have been better for him to have died three months ago. He had had a good life; this was a poor way to end it. Jeff turned and started away.

"Jeff, just a minute," Doc Hyman called.

He looked around and waited.

"I've heard what Grandy said to you," the doctor said. "If he was bitter and harsh, you can blame part of it on the constant pain he's suffered. Remember that."

"Sure, I'll remember it," Jeff said.

He walked on, trying to find some measure of understanding for Grandy in the last thing the doctor had said. But it was hard, and it didn't help. Grandy's bitterness was a hard thing to swallow.

CHAPTER 6

He had to be honest with Dan Hotchkiss. He was taking a job with him, but he didn't know how long he would stay, nor did he fully know the implications to Dan. If it was inevitable that he got in trouble with Doberman's crowd, he wasn't going to pull Dan into it. He wanted that clear. He was working here—and that was all.

Dan Hotchkiss, however, had a realistic way of looking at things. "Any of us can get in trouble with Doberman, any day," he said bluntly. "He's the kind to ask for it. The men riding for him are the same kind—quarrelsome, spoiling for a fight. I can smell it in the wind."

"But I don't want to be the cause of it," Jeff said.

"If it comes that way, it'll come. That's the kind of world we live in."

Harriet Hotchkiss was delighted by their new hand. If she felt any uneasiness, she hid it. And she didn't believe what Grandy had said. "He liked you too well," she insisted. "He's always liked you. When he comes to his senses, he'll send for you."

Jeff didn't argue the matter. He got to work the following day with Dan, and the next ten days were filled with activity. From dawn to dusk they kept busy. There was branding to be done and hay to be cut and gathered for winter feed. There were fences to be strengthened.

On the evening of the fourth day they had a visitor, Nels Gitterhaul. Having heard in town that Jeff was at the Hotchkiss ranch, he had come to see him. He sat down in the kitchen with Jeff, Dan and Harriet.

Nels was a big man, gruff and direct, and he seemed upset. "I don't believe what they're saying about Grandy," he said stubbornly. "I want you to see him again."

"Why?" Jeff asked.

"We need you in Doberman's place."

"Talk to my brother Wade."

"Wade! He's wrapped around Doberman's finger. He blusters and talks big, but he's a little man, even if he is your brother. I mean, half brother. What's wrong between you and Grandy?"

"I don't know, Nels."

"Could it be that story of what happened in Denver? They're saying you'll pay a thousand dollars to anyone who can prove it. They're also saying you won't have any takers. That story is pretty well exploded. Why don't you go see Grandy, and tell him?"

Jeff shook his head. "It was more than a rumor that made Grandy change his mind. He never put much stock in rumors."

"See him anyhow."

"I don't think it would do any good."

Nels sighed. "Someone's got to do something. Who knows what's next? Did you know Ben Adams?"

"Of course I know Ben."

"He's dead, Jeff. Vegas shot him two nights ago."

"Vegas! How did it happen?"

"They're saying, now, that Ben was drunk, that he started the fight and that he went for his gun before Vegas moved. But Ben wasn't the kind to get drunk. He wasn't the kind to start a fight. Anyhow, the story stood up. Vegas got free. And this is just an example of what to expect in the future if Doberman isn't stopped. Most of his men are gunslingers. They've got to keep in practice. There'll be others killed. I can see it."

The thought of Gwen flashed suddenly across Jeff's mind. She had been interested in Ben. How did she feel tonight? Empty? Numb? Shattered at what had happened? Crying, probably, but crying wouldn't help. Ben Adams was dead.

Harriet hadn't said anything, but she was watching her husband and she looked worried. Dan looked worried, too. And Nels seemed wholly baffled. He paced the floor, stirred up by his feelings.

"Jeff, what can we do?" he asked finally. "Damn it, what is there to do?"

"I don't know," Jeff admitted. "Wait, I suppose."

"Wait for what?"

"For whatever happens."

Four days later they had another visitor, this time a girl. She came late at night, hammering on the door. Dan met her with a gun in his hand. At the same time, Jeff was covering her from the darkness in the yard. They had heard a horse ride in, but they didn't know who had come.

"Hey, Jeff," Dan called from the door. "You have a guest. Gwen Sennett."

Jeff walked up to the house, trailing his rifle. He was surprised, and worried, too. Midnight was a strange hour for a visitor. "What's happened, Gwen?" he asked quickly.

"Nothing. But I had to see you."

"Come inside," Dan said.

"I don't want to wake the children, or Harriet."

"I'm already awake," Harriet called from within the house. "And don't worry about the children. An earthquake wouldn't jar them. I'll light the lamp."

They went inside. Gwen was in boots, jeans, a blouse and a sweater. Her hair had come loose and she raised her arms and was fooling with it, tightening it. She looked tired.

"I'll shake out the stove," Harriet said. "It won't take long to make coffee."

"No. Don't," Gwen said. "I must go back right away. It's a long ride, and we have to open the restaurant by dawn."

"That won't give you much time to sleep," Jeff said. "Can't your mother handle the restaurant in the morning?"

"She doesn't know I'm away. No one does. Are you going to town Saturday?"

Jeff looked at Dan, who bobbed his head. "Yes, we had planned on going to town Saturday. Need a few things."

"Then don't. That is—"

She broke off and glanced at Jeff, then looked away. Her face tightened, and her hands were clenched.

"You've heard something, haven't you?" Jeff said quietly.

"Yes, I have."

"What is it?"

She looked at him again. "I don't want you to go to town Saturday."

"Why, Gwen?"

"They're going to kill you. I don't know who's going to do it. I don't know how. I just know it's going to happen. You've got to stay away."

Gwen's words had come in a rush and in a high-pitched, strained voice. A sharp tension had gripped her, widening her eyes, stiffening her body. Harriet caught her breath. She stepped to her husband's side and gripped his arm. Dan was scowling.

Jeff walked to where Gwen was standing. He led her to a chair and made her sit down, then said, "Easy, Gwen. Nothing's happened yet. Rest for a minute."

She leaned back and closed her eyes. "Thanks, Jeff. I think I needed a chair. I'm—I'm frightened."

He dropped his hand on her shoulder. "There's nothing to be frightened about right now."

She looked up. "But Saturday—"

"It's not Saturday."

Harriet spoke positively. "I don't know how the rest of you feel, but I need coffee. I'm going to make it. And you men might get dressed."

Gwen told them, a little later, what she had heard. "A waitress hears things," she explained. "She can't help it. I get catches of conversations. Sometimes what I hear is quite clear. Sometimes it makes sense or sometimes you can put things together. What I've heard about you, Jeff, I've had to put together."

"Who did the talking?" Jeff asked.

"Different ones. Mr. Doberman, the one they call Vegas. A new man called Brick. Bill Traubert. And several more."

"They were talking about me."

"Yes. And they talked about Saturday. They

thought you might be in town Saturday. As I was passing the table once, Mr. Doberman said, 'If it's done the right way, the sheriff won't be able to do a thing.' Then Vegas said, later, 'Why not me? I never miss. With me, you'd be sure.' Then Brick said—he said—'Folks like him. Another killing won't help us.' Mr. Doberman told him to shut up. You believe me, don't you, Jeff?"

Jeff nodded. "Yes, I believe you."

"Then you won't go in Saturday?"

He smiled, dodging a direct answer. "It's something I'll have to think about. I'll have to go in someday. I can't go into hiding."

"Why not?" She straightened abruptly. "Why do you have to stay in the Park? Why not go away?"

"Maybe I like it here."

"But you don't have to go to town Saturday."

"No, I suppose you're right."

He turned away, crossed to the stove and stood there, puzzling over what Gwen had said. Actually, he wasn't greatly surprised. Brick had warned him to leave the Park. Wade had said the same thing. Doberman, too. They didn't want him here—but why? In more than a week he hadn't been near the Rocking H. He had taken another job, far away.

Dan said something to Harriet, then joined Jeff, and spoke under his breath. "If someone's after you, Jeff, why not out here? In the hills we've been working, there are a hundred places where you could have been ambushed."

"But that would be murder. In town, if they work it right, it can be made to look like a gunfight I provoked myself."

"What if you didn't wear a gun?"

"Too obvious. They'd try something else."

"Then how about if I stuck with you from the time you hit town?"

"And pull you down, too?"

"We might ride through it, Jeff."

"I don't know, Dan. We'll think about it."

The coffee was ready. They had it at the table, and afterwards Gwen got up to leave and Jeff went outside with her. There he mentioned Ben Adams, and was surprised at her answer.

"Don't feel too bad about me," she said, touching his arm lightly. "Ben was a fine man. I liked him, but I didn't love him. We wouldn't have been married. I thought about it—but only because I'm getting older. I'm almost twenty-three. A girl of twenty-three is supposed to have found a man."

"Then you haven't."

"I'm afraid not, Jeff."

He laughed softly. "You've plenty of time, Gwen. Don't rush it. I'll saddle up, then ride you to town."

· · ·

When Dan Hotchkiss was nineteen, eleven years before, only one thing in the world had been important. He had wanted some land, a place of his own. By the time he was twenty-three, he had managed it. He had bought his ranch. It was deeply in debt, but that hadn't worried him. Debts could be worked out.

Tonight, however, as he heard Jeff and Gwen ride off, he was worried. He knew things were wrong at the Rocking H. He knew that trouble was coming and that when it came it might touch him through Jeff. It was an escapable possibility. If he stuck to Jeff Saturday, there might be a shooting—and, if that happened, Saturday he might be dead. It wasn't a pleasant thing to contemplate. And he didn't have only himself to think about. The danger he felt stretched out to include Harriet and the children.

In a case such as this, where did a man's responsibilities lie? That was the question he had to answer. Did his loyalties belong wholly to his family, or did he have any others? Or he could put it in another way. In view of his family, did he have the right to endanger them? It was a tough problem.

"Let's have some more coffee, Harriet," he said gruffly. "I'll see how the children are."

He went to their room. All three children were asleep—Joe, who was five, Ed, almost four, and

Phyllis, the baby. He stood there and looked at them a moment, then walked back to the kitchen.

"You didn't need more coffee," Harriet said.

"I know."

She spoke from the wealth of understanding she had for the man she had married. "You are worried about Jeff, but that's not all. You're thinking of us."

"Shouldn't I, Harriet?"

"Yes—but we don't live alone in the world. Other people are here, too."

He stared at her thoughtfully. "What are you saying, dear? Spell it out."

"I don't have to. You know what's in your heart."

"You are there. And the children. And our land. Nothing else, Harriet."

She shook her head, smiling. "No, you're wrong. I wouldn't have married a man that selfish. Remember the blizzard last year? Who was it who almost lost his life searching for one of Nels' riders? Others gave up long before you."

"That was an emergency."

"What's this?"

Dan took a deep breath. "Then, Saturday in town, you'll have to take care of the children. If there's any shooting, I want you to stay right where you are. It won't be easy."

"Who said it was easy? Dan, I'll worry every

minute. I hate what you have to do. I want you to be safe—but I wouldn't have you a bit different. I—There's Phyllis."

The baby was awake, and she was hungry. She had a good pair of lungs, and, if she wasn't satisfied quickly, she would use them. They both knew it.

"Dinnertime again for Phyllis," she said smiling, starting for the bedroom.

"Harriet, you're a wonderful girl," Dan said feelingly, and he took a step toward her.

From the door she looked back, laughing softly. "The baby comes first. Afterwards, if you're still awake—"

"I'll be awake," Dan said.

To Jeff and Gwen, it was a pleasant night, clear and windless. As they cut across country, they talked. Gwen had spent the years before her father's death on a ranch, and she still remembered her years there, the dust of a drive and the smell of a branding fire. She knew how to use a rope and how to handle a gun. She loved riding, and she had kept it up.

Jeff kept the conversation going, but near the town they fell silent. The silence was broken suddenly by Gwen, who asked, directly, "Jeff, have you seen her since you got home?"

He looked surprised. How she had guessed he was thinking of Vicki he couldn't imagine. It made him abruptly self-conscious. "Yes, I've seen her," he admitted.

It was dark, but he still could see her frown. "What's wrong?"

"Nothing," he answered, growling the word. Then, for some reason or other, he added, "Vicki hasn't forgotten her brother's death."

"But that was an accident. You don't mean—"

"She was awfully close to her brother."

"But—"

She didn't finish the sentence, and again they were silent. When she spoke again, she changed the subject. "You'll be riding in to town Saturday, won't you?"

"Probably."

"Then my trip was for nothing."

"No. Not at all. I've been warned, Gwen. I'll be riding into town with my eyes wide open."

She looked straight at him. "If I was Vicki, I'd say, 'Ride away with me. Anywhere. Anywhere in the world.' "

"And I'd say, even to Vicki, that I couldn't."

"But you'll be careful?"

"Sure, I'll be careful."

They rode on. Jeff turned his thoughts toward Saturday. What would happen when he got to town? How careful could he be? In a situation such as this, what should a man do? That was a hard answer, and, actually, Saturday wasn't important. Doberman's plans for him were only one step in a pattern that still wasn't clear. What was his chief objective, and how did he mean to get there? That was what he had to find out. Maybe he ought to see Wade, or Syl. Preferably Syl. He would think about it on the way home.

CHAPTER 7

Harriet woke up the children earlier than usual Saturday morning, and was quite busy getting them ready for the trip to town. If she was at all worried, she hid it, but after they left she sat in the wagon with Dan and now and then reached for his hand. Jeff, riding near the wagon on the same horse he had borrowed from Will Shackle, noticed this, and noticed the way Dan instantly smiled at her when she touched him. The two boys rode in a second seat Dan had fixed up, and Harriet carried the baby. After an hour, Dan took her and Harriet drove the team.

Halfway in they stopped briefly in the shade of the trees along Deer Run creek, giving the two boys a chance to stretch their legs. Then, they rode on.

It was nearly eleven in the morning when they got to Crestline. By this time, several other wagons had made it to town and were hitched in the vacant space next to the bank. Jeff noticed Risling's wagon and, near it, Zeigler's. Harriet waved to the other women, then joined them as Dan unhitched the team. The boys had already climbed down and joined other children under the trees at the side. This was the normal procedure on Saturday, for Saturday was family day in Crestline, a day to bring in the women and children.

Jeff helped unhitch the team, then, with Dan, drove them to the rear of the lot and tied them. Other men were there—Ad Zeigler, John Risling, Nels Gitterhaul and a few more. Jeff knew everyone there. He spoke to several, sensing a vague uneasiness in the group. They knew, of course, that Grandy had disowned him and that he had gone to work for Dan; perhaps they didn't know what to say.

Dan was talking to Nels. Jeff waited and watched the horseshoe game that was in progress. But his mind wasn't on it. Driving through town he had noticed several Rocking H horses at the tie rail in front of the saloon, an indication that at least some of Doberman's crowd was here. In some way, then, as the day wore on, they would make their play. What it would be he couldn't guess. The simplest thing he could think of was a fight, one that was staged. But he had to expect anything.

"I've got to take an order to the grocery," Dan said, joining him. "Then we ought to return Will Shackle's horse and get yours. Want to go with me?"

Jeff shrugged. "Why not?"

"I think I'll tag along, too," Nels said.

It seemed like a casual offer, but Jeff was pretty

sure it wasn't at all casual. Dan had had a talk with Nels, undoubtedly telling him what might lie ahead. As a result, Jeff had two guards.

They returned Will Shackle's horse, picked up Jeff's and on the way back saw Art McEllis. He came to his door, waved and then called, "Jeff, I want to see you."

Dan glanced at Nels. "We'll wait outside."

"You don't have to watch me every minute," Jeff said. "And, if there's any trouble, just cover my back. That's all."

He turned toward the sheriff's office. He went inside, pushed back his hat, nodded and said, "Howdy, Sheriff."

"So you got your job," McEllis said sourly.

"Yep. I got a job."

"Staying with it?"

"Maybe."

The sheriff shook his head. "That's no answer, but we'll let it ride for a time. I get around. I hear things. What was the trouble you had in Indian Bluff with Bill Traubert?"

Jeff's interest sharpened. What was coming now? So far as he knew, he never had known anyone by that name, nor had he had any trouble in Indian Bluff. "Who's Traubert?" he asked bluntly.

"He's one of the new men working for Doberman. He came from Indian Bluff a day or so after you got here."

"Then he's new to me, too," Jeff said.

"Not as I get it. You and Traubert had a row, across the pass. What was it about?"

"Ask him."

McEllis thrust his head forward, his face reddening. "By God, I'm not gonna risk any trouble here. I want your gun."

"Did you get his?"

"Soon as I see him, I will."

"Then see him. Get him in and send for me. I'd like to meet him. I tell you I don't know him."

"I said I want your gun, Jeff."

"No."

They stood facing each other, silent for a moment. Here in the Park, men wore their guns. The sheriff could ask someone to give it up, but, unless he wanted to go all the way and make an arrest, he couldn't force it. Jeff was aware of that, and so was the sheriff. He had tried to run a bluff. Now he had to back down, and it wasn't easy. "All right. Keep your gun," he said finally. "But if there's any trouble, if there's any shooting at all, someone's gonna spend the night in jail."

Jeff turned away and stepped outside to join the two men who had been waiting.

"Did you hear what was said?" Jeff asked.

"Most of it," Dan said.

"Who's Traubert?"

"I've seen him once or twice," Nels said. "He's about average-sized, walks with a lurch.

He's sort of a dandy. Dresses up, fancy vests. Could be a gunslinger."

"He would be if they've picked him," Dan said.

Jeff looked up and down the street. Here and there a few people were in sight, but he didn't see any of Doberman's crowd. He would see them, however, and he could imagine what was ahead. A ready-made quarrel had been set up. Back in Indian Bluff, he and Traubert were supposed to have had trouble. Today their fictitious argument could be settled, and, if it resulted in his death, it would seem to have nothing to do with Doberman or the Rocking H.

"No sense in rushing into a gunfight," Dan muttered.

"No sense at all," Nels agreed. "But what'll we do?"

"We'll wait for the next move," Jeff said. "Let's see what happens."

They stopped at the grocery where Dan left his list; then they walked on to the bank lot. It was time for dinner. The restaurant was already well filled, but a few tables were still free. They took one, Jeff sitting with Dan's family. Nels took another with his wife and the Rislings.

Gwen served them. She was terribly busy, and seemed tense. As she gave Jeff his plate she whispered, "Matt Doberman and two of his men were in earlier for coffee. They said—"

She suddenly froze, staring toward the door. Jeff looked that way. Five men had just come in. Three he knew—Doberman, Brick, and his brother Wade. The other two were strangers. One was wearing a fancy vest, white silk decorated with black embroidery. A few others in the room were wearing fancy vests, but they couldn't compare with this one.

"I reckon you can pick out Traubert," Dan said under his breath.

The five men were making their way to a vacant table. Doberman, leading the way, spoke genially to several people as he passed. Wade looked stiff and nervous, while Brick appeared wholly unconcerned. Jeff hardly noticed the fourth man because he was watching Traubert. Suddenly Traubert stopped and stared at him. His face was slightly flushed, perhaps from drinking, but his eyes were steady and hard. The man stood motionless until Doberman called to him to come on and sit down.

Then someone else came in—the sheriff. He didn't sit at one of the tables, but took a position against the wall, near the door, and stood there.

The room had been noisy a few minutes before, but now a hush fell across it. Some of those present knew the reason, and others may have guessed it. Jeff glanced at Harriet. Her face had paled, and she was looking at Dan.

"We'll go on with our meal," she said steadily.

Dan nodded. "Sure we will. Isn't that why we came here?"

The next half hour wasn't comfortable. Several families hurried through their food and left. At the Rocking H table, Wade found several things to say to Doberman and Brick talked to the fourth man. Traubert was silent. His back was to Jeff, but occasionally he took a look over his shoulder. The sheriff held his station at the door. Why he was there was obvious—he wanted no trouble here in the restaurant where others might be hurt.

Jeff finished his meal. He pushed back his plate and said, "Dan, I'll go outside first."

"No, we'll go together," Dan said. "Harriet can remain with the children."

"I'm through, too," the oldest boy said.

"Then you can take care of your mother," Dan said.

Harriet's hand was shaking as she reached for a glass of water, but her voice was even. "We'll be all right, Dan."

Jeff glanced toward the Rocking H table. Traubert had jerked around to stare at him. He looked as though he were about to stand up, but then something else happened. Gwen, hurrying past the Rocking H table with a tray of dishes, seemed to trip and lose her balance. She spilled the tray almost into Traubert's lap. Something on it must have been hot, for Traubert jumped to his feet, shouting hoarsely and brushing his hands on his vest and pants. The others at the table got up quickly. Wade looked startled, and Doberman, too. But Brick was laughing.

"Why don't you look where you're goin'!" Traubert roared. "Look what you done to my clothes!"

His fancy vest was ruined, splashed with coffee, gravy and particles of food. The front of his pants was soaked.

"I'm awfully sorry," Gwen said.

Traubert glared at her. He drew back his fist, but Brick caught his arm and held it. "Just simmer down," he said, still laughing. "It was an accident. Didn't hurt you, anyhow."

During the confusion around the Rocking H table, Jeff left the restaurant, accompanied by Dan and Nels. They walked on to the bank lot, and no one followed them. Traubert might have, but, if he had meant to, Gwen had prevented it.

Dan laughed all the way to the lot. "It certainly was no accident," he claimed. "I saw exactly what happened. Gwen was hanging back, waiting for the right moment. She pitched the tray right into Traubert's lap, a hot pot of coffee with it."

"A neat bit of acting," Nels agreed. "I'll bet the middle of Traubert's body is still on fire. His pants were a mess, and that fancy vest will never be the same."

Jeff grinned. Damned if Gwen wasn't quite a girl. She had planned this on her own, and what she had done had been quite effective. Maybe she hadn't stopped Traubert completely, but she had upset him and made him look ridiculous. It was hard to look grim and dangerous with people laughing, and that was what had happened.

Down the street at the restaurant, the sheriff came outside with the Rocking H riders. They stood talking for a time, and the sheriff seemed to be doing most of it. Then after a time Doberman's men walked on to the saloon. There they talked for a while longer, but finally one of them mounted his horse and wheeled out of town. It was Bill Traubert.

"Didn't have another clean vest," Dan said, amused. "I knew of a gunslinger who had a special hat. It was old and battered, but if he was expecting trouble he always wore it. Had a good hat, too. One day he ran into an enemy and had his good hat on. He tried to stall the fight until he could change hats, but he couldn't. As he was dying he didn't blame the other man. Blamed not having his old hat. Maybe Traubert's that way with vests. At least, he's gone."

There wasn't much question of that. The sheriff waited until Traubert left town, then walked to the bank lot.

"Traubert's gone," he said flatly. "Now, I reckon we can rest easy, no thanks to you, Jeff."

"I told you before I don't know the man," Jeff said. "I wouldn't have started anything."

McEllis shrugged and said, "Jeff, next time I'll look the other way. Next time it's your own funeral."

"Or Traubert's."

"Or both of yours. Damn it, Jeff, what are you holding out for? Wade says he thinks you've got a notion you'll get a chunk of Grandy's range after he dies. I can tell you right now you won't. Grandy's made a new will, splitting his land between Wade and Syl. You're not even mentioned."

"Then I won't get anything."

"You're staying here, anyhow?"

"I like it here."

McEllis shook his head hopelessly. He glanced at Dan and then at Nels. He was scowling, but behind it was uncertainty.

"If I were you," Nels said, "I wouldn't worry about Jeff. I'd worry about the kind of men Doberman's brought to the Park. Take what happened when Vegas shot Ben Adams. A thing like that—"

"Had a talk with Doberman," the sheriff said, interrupting. "He's going to keep his men in line."

"He didn't do anything to keep Traubert in line."

"The hell he didn't. He just sent Traubert home, didn't he?"

Jerking away, the sheriff stalked toward his office. They watched him for a time; then Nels made a thoughtful observation. "McEllis wants to play it straight, but his feelings get in the way. He never did like you, did he, Jeff?"

"No, I'm afraid you're right."

"And on the other hand, he likes Doberman. Don't know why, but he does. A man can overlook a lot of things for a friend."

Harriet had some errands. While she took care of them, Dan checked at the grocery. Then reported that they could leave in about an hour.

"Then I think I'll see Gwen," Jeff said. "I want to thank her."

"That ought to be safe enough," Dan said. Then he added, "Vicki's in town."

Jeff hadn't seen her. He wanted to, but he didn't notice her along the street and when he got to the restaurant he went inside. Dinner was over. Gwen and her mother were in the kitchen cleaning up. They looked around as he came in, and Mrs. Sennett said, "They tell me I have a very awkward daughter, Jeff."

"A terribly awkward daughter," Jeff said, laughing.

"I tripped," Gwen said. "I was quite embarrassed."

She didn't look it, however. Her eyes were bright, and she was having a hard time keeping a straight face.

Mrs. Sennett dried her hands. She said, "You finish here, Gwen. I'll start in the front room. Watch the fire in the stove."

"What can I do?" Jeff asked.

"You can help dry the dishes," Gwen said. "You might as well get some practice. If you ever get married, that's one thing you'll have to learn."

Jeff got to work, grumbling about it but not meaning it. Gwen seemed amused. She added wood to the firebox, peeked at the pies in the oven and then stirred something on the stove and moved it to the back.

"Do you have to work all the time?" Jeff asked.

"No. In about an hour we'll be done here. But by then folks will be dropping in for coffee, and soon after that it'll be the supper hour. We manage to keep busy."

"Every day?"

"For me, every day until I get married. Then Mother will have to find someone to take my place."

"Then if I were you I'd get married."

"Should I? Really?"

"If you can find the man—go after him."

"No matter who he is?"

"If you want him, yes. Go after him and get him."

Gwen turned from the stove, and possibly it was the heat that made her cheeks so pink.

"I may do it," she said. "I may really go after him."

Jeff had finished drying the remaining dishes. He hung up the towel and said, "Gwen, I don't know how to thank you for what you did. If I knew—"

"Just keep alive," Gwen answered. "There will be other Trauberts. Are you going to stay with Dan?"

"Until I can see through Doberman's plan. He's got one, Gwen. When Grandy dies the ranch will go to Wade and Syl. But that won't give Doberman the control he needs. Maybe he could win Wade's share in a gambling game, but what about Syl? She's still in the way, and she can be awfully stubborn."

"Suppose she got married?"

"Syl? She'd never marry a man like Doberman."

"But how about the new man? He was at the table today."

"Brick Rawson!"

"Why not, Jeff. He's young, good-looking. He's got a grin you can't miss. How well do you know your sister?"

"She's never looked at a man."

Gwen looked skeptical. "You don't know women at all. Maybe Syl hasn't seemed interested in men, but she's seen them, measured them. All women do. And this Brick Rawson rates above the average."

Jeff was silent for a moment. What Gwen had suggested hadn't occurred to him before, but why wasn't it a possibility? Brick had come here as a result of a letter from Doberman. He might be a gunslinger, but beyond that he was a man who was personally attractive to women. Actually, Doberman didn't need more gunslingers, but maybe he needed someone who could influence Syl. That could have been Brick's job.

"Well, Jeff?" Gwen asked quietly.

"You've given me something to think about, anyhow."

"At least that's something."

He scarcely noticed her comment. He still was thinking of Brick and Syl. If something happened to Wade, and if Syl and Brick got married, then who would be running the Rocking H? Why, Syl's husband—or Doberman—or perhaps the two together.

"Jeff?" Gwen was saying.

He looked at her abruptly. "What is it?"

"Just because Bill Traubert left town is no reason to coast."

"I'll be careful," he said, grinning. "Good luck, too."

"Good luck about what?"

"In getting that man."

She sighed hopelessly. "I'm afraid I don't have a chance."

"Keep working."

He stepped forward, reached for her hands and squeezed them. Then he leaned forward and kissed her. It had been an entirely impulsive thing, and he didn't mean it to be anything more. But it didn't work out that way. Gwen's arms came up around his shoulders and tightened. Her lips touched his. They were warm, and soft, and clinging. He sensed the pressure of her breasts and then became aware of the full length of her young, vibrant body, strong against him. He was shaky when he pushed away; he couldn't think, and his breath was coming fast. His face was red, too—he could feel its heat.

He said, "Gwen—Gwen—" And didn't know what to say next.

"That's all right," she answered. "But you'd better go. Mother might come in."

He twisted away. He needed to get away, quickly. He felt terribly confused.

"Jeff?" she called as he reached the door.

He looked around. She seemed wholly composed. She was even smiling. He asked, "What is it, Gwen."

"Think about it."

He didn't answer her. He was already angry at what he had done, or at what she had done. Think about it? Why? What was there to think about? The thing to do was forget it. That was what he would do.

CHAPTER 8

Matt Doberman was nursing his second drink. Right after dinner he had had a quick drink; he had needed it. But he was being careful of his second. He knew his own habits. If he took a second, and then two more, he would be ready to hit someone, and that wouldn't be wise. Here in the Park he was playing for high stakes. He needed a clear head.

Creel came in, joined him and then spoke under his breath. "Jeff Carmody's still in town. He's at the restaurant. No one's watching him. Vegas an' me could frame a fight. Should be easy."

"Not a chance," Doberman whipped back. "Quit pushing me. It wouldn't look right, no matter how you set it up. Keep out of Jeff's way."

He took another sip of the drink, then sat there silently. A plan had gone wrong, but what of it? He could set up another, one that could fit neatly into the old framework and that would be even stronger. He considered it for a time, checking every angle. He was feeling much better when he left the saloon and hunted up the sheriff.

"Been thinking, Sheriff," he said slowly and with apparent honesty. "I don't like it, having a man on the Rocking H who's gunning for Jeff. It doesn't look right. After all, if Jeff had behaved himself, he'd still be home."

"That's not your problem," McEllis said.

"Maybe not, but it still ain't right to have a man on the Rocking H who's gunning after Jeff. I'm going to fire Traubert. Kick him out."

"I'd say that was damned white."

"Forget it. I'm still worried about Jeff. Wade's sure he'll make trouble."

"How can he? Jeff's out. How you getting along with Wade?"

Doberman shrugged. "He's a good kid. Young. But he'll learn, Sheriff. I get rough with him sometimes, but I have to. We get along. Be seeing you."

He turned away, quite satisfied with the conversation. He had a good ally in McEllis, and it didn't cost anything. Across the street Brick was mounting his horse. Doberman shouted to him, then walked in that direction, suddenly angry. "Where the hell do you think you're going?" he asked bluntly.

Brick grinned. "The show's over. Syl's back at the ranch. I'm going home."

"Anything new?"

"Nope."

"You haven't done a lick of work. You've been spending a lot of time with her. What the hell's been happening?"

"With Syl it takes time," Brick answered. "I know what I'm doing."

"I wish I was sure of it."

Brick shrugged and said nothing.

Doberman stared at the man thoughtfully. He was uneasy about Brick, and had felt that way since his arrival. Why he didn't know. Certainly, from what Brick had said, he had no reasons to complain. The man knew why he was here, what he had to do. He had agreed to take the job. In the face of that, then, why did he feel uncertain about him?

"Brick, I want you to hurry it," he said abruptly.

The man scowled. "Why? We agreed we wouldn't rush things."

"I didn't say you could take your time, either. I'll give you another week."

"Two weeks."

"One."

Brick leaned toward him. "All right, I'll try. But I may need more time, and if I do I'll take it. Don't get in a panic just because Fancy Vest Traubert made a fool of himself."

He didn't wait for a reply but, wheeling away, galloped his horse up the street.

Doberman swore under his breath. Then, over at the corner of the saloon, he noticed Vegas and he was able to smile. Why was he worried about Brick? He would do his job; then, shortly afterwards, he wouldn't be necessary. When that day came, Vegas could be used. No one he knew could stand up against Vegas.

He went back to the saloon, took a table alone and had another drink. Now he half regretted telling Brick to hurry. Actually, there was no hurry at all. This operation required time. If it was hurried, it wouldn't look good. Every week that passed put him more solidly in the saddle. Wade was a problem. It was hard to put up with him, but he had to. He needed to be pictured as a loyal foreman, correcting Wade's errors, working hard to hold the ranch together, with no thought of himself. This was a curious role he was taking. It made him want to laugh out loud.

After a while he went outside and spent the rest of the afternoon drifting up and down the street, talking to everyone he knew. He was as friendly as he could be, and quite modest, too. He had praise for Wade. To a few people he deplored the break between Grandy and Jeff. He tried this on Abe Waldron and his daughter. Abe had little to say, but Vicki seemed interested.

Right after supper he rode home. He got there well before midnight. Brick and Syl, of course, had gone somewhere, and Paul Lanier, who had been left in charge, said everything was quiet. He sent Lanier back to the bunkhouse; then, with the house to himself, he walked to Grandy's room, struck a match and lit the lamp. Grandy lay motionless in his bed, apparently asleep.

Doberman spoke quietly. "Wake up, old man. I want to talk to you."

Grandy still seemed asleep.

"Old man, we almost took care of Jeff today. A fool waitress got in the way, but next time we won't miss."

Grandy's eyes opened, but he didn't speak.

"We're sending Traubert against him," Doberman said. "You never saw anyone fast as Traubert."

"If they meet, Jeff will kill him," Grandy said.

"Like hell. Jeff's as good as dead. Now, what I want to know is this. How long are you going to hang on?"

Grandy's eyes had closed again, but at that last question he opened them again. "I'll hang on," he said weakly. "I'll hang on until I can get out of bed and kill you."

His feeble defiance was really funny. Doberman threw back his head and roared. Quite often, late at night, he came here to Grandy's room and talked this way if no one else was around. Grandy had been a well-established cattleman, a man who gave orders, important in the community. Doberman hated him for it. He liked to see the old man squirm, and he had him right where he wanted. In one hand he held the lives of Wade and Syl. In the other he held Grandy's. He was in an impregnable position. Grandy had to say what he told him to, or someone would die. It was as simple as that.

"Old man, your daughter's off with one of my men," he said abruptly. "He'll handle her, just the way I say. Wade's no problem at all. Everything's going fine. Hang on for a while—but not too long. I could snuff out your life in a minute."

Grandy's eyes had closed again. He seemed, right then, very near death. He was terribly thin, his color was bad and he was too weak to turn in bed. Only a glimmer of his spirit still lived.

"Good night, old man," Doberman said. "Dream of all the acres you're leaving me."

Grandy said nothing.

Jeff stood it for two more days at the ranch, but the following morning he told Dan he had to take some time off. He had been thinking of Brick and his sister. He wanted to see her, or even Wade. It was all right to wait, but a man couldn't wait forever.

"I want to talk to Syl," he explained to Dan. "She's been left alone, with no one to talk to, unless it's Brick Rawson. She was pretty rough on me when I arrived at the Rocking H, but we used to get along rather well. Maybe I could get somewhere with her."

"But how will you get to her?" Dan asked. "It may not be easy."

"No, it shouldn't be at all hard. She rides out alone. Always has. I'll head for town and stand watch."

"What if you run into Traubert?"

"I'll dodge him. I won't go to town. I'll watch the road."

Dan offered no other objections. He seemed to sense Jeff's need to do something. "I've really been working you," he said, grinning. "Maybe you've earned a vacation. But don't take chances. Play it safe."

Jeff left the next morning, carrying several days' supplies with him, in case he needed them. He might find Syl before dark, but, on the other hand, it might take a couple of days. He didn't know exactly what to expect.

Shortly before noon he settled down in the shelter of the trees fringing the river, west of town. There he had a view of the road to the Rocking H. Toward mid-afternoon, Doberman came in sight. Four others were with him, but Syl wasn't one of them. He remembered that in the past she had ridden to town almost every day. If she was still doing it, she might come by. He was counting on it, and finally he saw her. But she wasn't alone—Brick was with her.

They were traveling slowly, talking and obviously enjoying themselves. He couldn't hear their laughter, but he could sense it. Jeff watched them, feeling distinctly uneasy. Syl needed a man—someone who could excite her, bring color to her face, make her laugh. But not a man who would break her heart. Not a man who meant to use her. Not Brick Rawson.

Jeff stayed where he was, struggling with the problem of what to do about them. If Syl had fallen in love with Brick, it wasn't going to be easy to talk to her. She might hate him for it, might not listen at all. This was a ticklish matter. And, if they could handle Syl through Brick, how would they handle Wade? His brother was possibly in grave danger. Damn it, he had to talk to Syl, no matter the cost to himself.

It grew dark, and Jeff had a cold supper. He was afraid he wasn't getting any place. If Syl had ridden to town, they would return together. Of course, he could go to town and insist on seeing his sister, but such a talk would be hurried and unsatisfactory. He might run into trouble, too—Traubert might be there. He wouldn't gain a thing if he got in a fight.

Then another possibility hit him. He knew the Rocking H as he knew his own hand. He knew the buildings and the surrounding area. There were two dogs at the ranch, but both knew him and neither would bark. He knew where he could leave his horse, near the ranch. He knew the way to Syl's room. He could go there, silently as a shadow. Then, why not try it? Once he was there, Syl wouldn't betray him. Of that he was sure.

The more he thought of it, the better he liked it. And such a step was necessary if he wanted to see his sister alone. It was a dangerous thing to do, maybe, but if he was careful he should be able to get there and get away again without being seen.

He started directly for the Rocking H, following the road, and he held it as far as the Bear Trap crossing. From there, either the road or the creek would have taken him to the ranch, but instead he cut across country. In an hour and a half he was in sight of Sentinel Hill, a rocky knoll that rose due west of the ranch buildings. His mother had been buried up there, and soon, probably, it would become Grandy's final resting place.

Jeff half circled the hill, and then left his horse in the timber on its far slope. From there he walked the good mile distance to the ranch. Near the main building, dim lamplight showed at the parlor windows and from the bunkhouse, but the place seemed quiet. Probably several men had been left at home, and were still up. He wasn't worried, however. It wasn't likely anyone expected visitors.

No one challenged him as he gained the porch. He listened at the door but could hear nothing. He stepped to one of the windows. A slight tear in the shade gave him a glimpse of the interior, and he was instantly glad he hadn't tried the door. Someone was inside, sprawling in one of the chairs, dozing. The big man he had noticed the morning he and Brick arrived.

What had been his name? Lanier. Paul Lanier.

Jeff stepped away. He realized now he should have expected to find someone inside. Lanier was in a chair near the west wing corridor. He was there, undoubtedly, to take care of Grandy, should he awake and need something.

One of the dogs found him in the dark shadows close to the house. He came up growling but wagging his tail. Jeff petted the dog, then moved along the wall of the house to Syl's room. The window was screened, but half open. He had to tear the screen to unlock it, but after that it wasn't hard to climb inside and pull the screen into position. Then he had nothing to do but wait.

It was after midnight before Syl and Brick got back from town. Jeff heard them in the yard, then a few minutes later heard Syl come in and dismiss Lanier. "I'll take care of my father if he calls," she told him. "The others will be home in a few minutes. Did Wade get in?"

"Not yet," Lanier said.

"Then he's still with Vicki," Syl said, sounding pleased.

Then Jeff heard her footsteps in the corridor, but she didn't come directly to her room. Instead she walked on to Grandy's room, undoubtedly to check on him. After that, she returned, entered her room and walked to the dresser to light the lamp. She was humming under her breath.

Jeff stood waiting. Lamplight suddenly flooded the room, and she turned and saw him. She must have recognized him immediately, but still a startled gasp broke from her throat and she raised her hands to her breasts, her eyes widening.

"It's just me," Jeff said quietly.

She looked quickly at the door. "What are you doing here?"

"Just came to see you."

"If they find you, they'll kill you."

"Why, Syl? Why should anyone want to kill me?"

"There's a man here named Bill Traubert. If he sees you—"

Jeff stared at her soberly. "Is he the only one I have to worry about?"

"Isn't that enough?"

"How's Grandy?"

Her eyes sharpened. "If you came here to bother my father—"

"But I didn't, Syl. If Grandy feels as he says, I don't want the ranch or any part of it. Really, I mean it. He seems to hate me, and maybe he does. I can't change the way I feel, however. He once was my father. Tell me how he is."

Syl bit her lips. She closed the door, then walked to the window and drew the shade. Her face had altered. She suddenly looked terribly tired, worried. "He's dying, Jeff. Dying by inches and fighting it all the way. I can sense it. He's terribly weak. The pain in his chest never stops. I—I almost wish he was dead. Is that a horrible thing to say?"

"No, Syl. It isn't."

"I stay with him as much as I can, but I don't believe he wants me there. He won't talk. He's saving his strength. He thinks he's going to get well, that the pain will pass, and that someday he'll get up and walk out, just like old times. Of course, he won't. He doesn't have a chance."

"How does Wade take it?"

"He's sorry, but he acts like—I don't want to talk about him."

"He likes being boss," Jeff said, guessing at what was in Syl's mind.

"He's—very young."

Jeff shrugged and changed the subject. "I want to talk about something else. It's not going to be easy. That is—"

"You want to talk about Brick," she said directly.

"How did you guess?"

A curious expression crossed her face. "Maybe I know you—big brother."

"I don't want to act like a big brother."

She looked straight at him. "You're going to tell me that Brick's a gunslinger, and that he's been an outlaw. You're going to say he was brought here to make love to me and to marry me. And you're probably going to say he's had a dozen other women."

Jeff was amazed at her perception. He didn't know what to expect next. "I wouldn't have put it that bluntly," he said.

"But you could have."

"Yes. I think I could."

Syl walked to the bed. She sat down, folded her hands in her lap and stared at the floor. "Yes, Brick is all I said. A gunslinger, an outlaw. He came here to marry me, not because I was beautiful or because he loved me, but because someday I'll own a part of the Rocking H range. He's had other women—but I don't care. I don't care what he's been, or why he came. I'm going to marry him."

Jeff stirred restlessly. "Why?"

"Because I love him."

She looked up, tears suddenly flooding her eyes. Her face looked tortured. Jeff had never seen her with such an expression—fear was there, and desperation, and a driving recklessness. Her breath was coming faster, and her hands were locked together.

"There's not much I can say, is there?" he asked.

"Nothing you can say would make me change my mind."

"Then what about Wade?"

"I don't care about Wade."

"Have you taken a good look at Doberman?"

"Matt Doberman. What does he have to do with it?"

"Suppose we figure it out," he said slowly. "Right now, Doberman's riding high. He's got a hand-picked crowd. He's letting Wade act like a boss, but what will happen after Grandy dies? The ranch, then, will belong half to you, half to Wade. If you and Brick get married, Doberman will be able to control your part of the ranch through your new husband. But what of Wade? How will they handle him? One way would be to kill him. If that happened, his share would go to you. Then, Doberman would have everything."

She came gradually to her feet, her cheeks colorless. "They wouldn't do anything to Wade. Why should they? He does what they say. He wouldn't be in the way."

"He's not in the way now. But he could be. He likes authority. He likes to wave a stick and give orders. At the present, Doberman is taking it, but he doesn't like it. Wade is in real danger."

She didn't question what he had said. She seemed to understand, and she stepped over quickly and grasped his arm. "Jeff, what can we do?"

"I don't know. You can't talk to Wade. He wouldn't listen."

"Would it help if I—if I refused to get married."

"Yes, that would help—but that in itself isn't

enough. I don't have a solution. I'm hunting for one."

Syl brushed her hands over her head. She turned to the dresser and stood there for a moment, peering at her reflection in the mirror. A shudder ran over her, and she said, "Jeff, I don't know what I'll do. I want to think. I wish— I wish we were all children again. It was good in those days. If we could only turn back—but we can't turn back, can we?"

"No, Syl. One of the rude facts of life is that we have to grow up."

"If we—"

She broke off what she was saying and raised her head, listening. A number of riders had pulled into the yard and were dismounting. Jeff could hear their voices faintly.

"That's the men back from town," Syl said. "Jeff, you should have left sooner."

"I'll make it," Jeff said.

Syl blew out the lamp. She crossed to the window, raised the window and then stood peering into the darkness. Her room was on the side away from the yard where the men were dismounting. There wasn't much chance anyone would come around here.

Jeff stepped up behind her and touched her shoulder. "Syl, I wish things could be different."

She looked around. "How about you and Vicki?"

"I haven't had a real chance to see her."

"Wade's been spending a lot of time over there."

"So I've heard."

"I don't know if it means anything or not. Wade started going because of you. He took your place with Grandy. He wanted to do the same with Vicki. He's changed, Jeff. He hardly talks to me any more. I think he hates you."

"He always has," Jeff said. "It goes far back. It started when it seemed to him as though Grandy favored me, but that wasn't true. I liked the things Grandy did. Wade didn't."

She stood listening, then nodded. "The men have gone in. I can hear them in the kitchen. You'd better go, Jeff."

He knew she was right. He had stayed longer than he should have. Passing her, he pushed out the screen, then climbed outside and dropped to the ground. He swept his eyes from side to side. He could see no movement in the shadows.

"Jeff?" she whispered from the room.

"What is it, Syl?"

"I don't know what I'll do about Brick. I don't want to lose him. You don't know how I feel inside. Now, don't say anything back. I want to make up my own mind."

He heard her lock the screen, then lower the window halfway. Standing close to the wall of the building, he again searched the shadows. Nothing moved, and no foreign sounds alarmed him. A slight breeze stirred through the air. From some far distant point he heard the wavering cry of a coyote. In the corral the horses were stirring around, but the noise would soon fade. He could sense no danger. He should have no trouble getting away.

He started off, slanting toward Sentinel Hill, but he had taken only a few steps before things began to happen. At the back corner of the house he heard a scraping sound. He jerked his head that way and dropped to the ground instantly, drawing his gun. Back there at the corner, a lumpy shadow had moved. Jeff held his breath and lay motionless, every muscle rigid. Who had he seen at the corner? What was the man doing there? What had he seen?

A voice spoke suddenly, not loud but clearly. "On your feet, Jeff. Shove your hands in the air. You're covered from four points."

Jeff still hugged the ground. He turned his head from side to side. At first he could spot only the man who had spoken; then at the front corner of the house another shadow moved, and in the glistening starlight he caught a flashing reflection from a rifle barrel.

"On your feet, Jeff," the man ordered again. "You've got no cover. We've got you boxed. Get on your feet and shove your hands above your head."

It was dark, but not dark enough. Two men were covering him, and there could easily be more. He could make a break for Sentinel Hill, but there was a good chance he wouldn't make it. There was no cover in the next quarter of a mile. He was as good as caught.

The order came once more. "On your feet, Jeff. Last chance. On your feet."

There was no help for it. Jeff stood up, holstered his gun and raised his arms above his head. The two shadowy figures he had spotted moved toward him. And there were two more, one from each side. He stood motionless, waiting for them, wondering how they had known he was here. But that was unimportant. The vital question now was what they would do.

One of the four men was Brick, and one was Vegas. The other two he didn't recognize. It was Brick who was running things.

"Get his gun, Vegas," he ordered.

"Would have saved us trouble if we'd shot him," Vegas growled. But he took Jeff's gun, then backed away.

Brick pushed back his hat, undoubtedly grinning. He said, "Sorry, Jeff, but you just didn't use your head." Then his voice changed and he snapped, "Take him to the barn. I'll get Doberman."

CHAPTER 9

They took him to the barn, and they weren't gentle about it. They tied his hands behind his back, then lashed him to one of the uprights supporting the hayloft. Then they lit lanterns and hung them on some of the other uprights. After this they stood and waited.

Traubert came in, this time wearing a red vest trimmed in blue. He looked excited. He said, "Caught you sooner than I thought."

"We had no trouble in Indian Bluff," Jeff said.

"Sure we didn't," Traubert said, grinning. "And I didn't need the story. That was Doberman's idea."

Jeff heard voices in the yard, and a moment later Doberman came in, flanked by Brick, his brother Wade and Paul Lanier. Doberman looked highly pleased, and Wade's face was flushed with excitement. He had been saying something when they came in, but Doberman had cut him off with an order to shut up. Brick's expression was unreadable, and this time his ironic smile was missing. Lanier was grinning.

"Knew you'd show up," Doberman said. "Expected it. Wasn't it enough when Grandy threw you out? Why did you want to bust in again? What did you think you would get out of it?"

"I didn't come here to see Grandy," Jeff said.

"Like hell."

Jeff shook his head. "I didn't go near my father. Ask Syl."

Wade leaned forward. "By God, he's not your father. He kicked you out."

"Sure he did," Jeff said flatly.

Doberman said, "Brick, go see what Syl's got to say. And don't take all night."

"Be right back," Brick said, whirling away.

Wade didn't seem to like what was happening. He waved his arm with a sweeping motion. "Why bring Syl into it? She's always been soft about Jeff. She'll try to save him."

"Shut up," Doberman snapped.

As though grated to the raw, Wade whipped around to face Doberman. "You can't talk to me like that. I'll not shut up. I'm giving the orders."

A moment of silence followed as everyone stared at the two men. Doberman's hand dropped toward his gun, but he didn't touch it. His face got red, and he seemed to be fighting some private war within himself. He spoke finally, his words gruff, placating, but still with an edge. "Wade, in ranch matters you're boss, but this is different. Keeping order is part of my job. Let me handle it my own way. I want to find out what Syl's got to say. I didn't say I'd believe it."

This was half a victory for Wade, and he

seemed satisfied. He had asserted himself. He laughed too loudly and glanced imperiously at the others. "Sure, Doberman. We understand each other. We'll stick together all the way."

Jeff wondered if his brother had any notion how close he had been to death.

Brick returned surprisingly soon. "I've talked to Syl," he reported. "She said Jeff didn't try to see Grandy. He wanted to see her."

"Why?"

"She wouldn't tell me. She said it was a private matter."

"Private, hell," Doberman grated. He twisted around toward Jeff. "What was the private matter?"

Jeff knew that nothing he said would be satisfactory. To tell the truth would be a sentence to death, and anything else would sound too weak to be realistic. He said, stoically, "Syl is my sister. We talked about a private matter. I can't repeat it. If you—"

Doberman leaned forward. His hand slashed out and caught Jeff across the face, bringing tears to his eyes and making his ears ring. His nose started bleeding. He could feel the thick taste of the blood in his mouth, could feel it dripping over his chin.

"Traubert," Doberman said suddenly. "Do you want to settle your fight with Jeff?"

Traubert nodded. "Sure I do."

"Then cut his hands free. Take that rope from around him and give him his gun."

Brick started laughing. He said, "Doberman, I'll give you odds—ten to one on Jeff. Any amount you want."

"Damn you, Brick," Traubert shouted hoarsely. "I'll call that bet myself."

"You won't be here," Brick answered. "Ask Wade about his brother."

Traubert was furious. "To hell with what you heard. Maybe you think you're good yourself?"

Doberman shoved between the two men. He glared at Brick. "What are you trying to do? Haven't you got any sense at all?"

"Sure I do," Brick said. "I don't like what's happening. If Jeff gets killed here, it isn't going to look good. In town it was different. It would be a gunfight. If it happens here, it could start a lot of ugly rumors."

"I suppose you'd let him go."

"Nope, but how about using Paul Lanier? Jeff wouldn't be much of a danger to us after Lanier worked him over. Did you ever see him fight?"

Doberman's eyes narrowed. He seemed to be considering what Brick had said. He glanced at Lanier, who had shoved forward, his simple grin widening. Lanier raised his fists as a challenge. They were huge, scarred from other battles.

"I say, leave things as they were," Traubert shouted. "We made a deal, Doberman."

"Cut it out, Traubert," Doberman snapped. "You can earn extra money some other way. I want to see Lanier work."

Jeff had been untied, but he hadn't been given a gun. Now he wasn't going to get one. Now he had to fight Lanier.

He stared at the man. Lanier was big, but he wasn't all bulk. His forearms were well-corded and he had powerful shoulders. Maybe he was slow, but Jeff couldn't count on it. It wasn't true that all big men were slow. Some were amazingly quick.

There was another thing to remember, too. A fist fight could be a grim and bloody affair. It could end in death. Once he had seen a man cut to ribbons by bruising fists, then die from a boot kick in the head. In that fight, nothing had been barred. And nothing would be barred tonight.

Jeff stood rooted where he was, watching Lanier. How did you fight a giant like this? One good solid blow from Lanier's fist would lift him off his feet and hurl him to the floor. If he didn't get up immediately, a boot would get him.

The others had drawn back to give them room. At one side Doberman spoke up. "Fifty dollars Jeff doesn't last five minutes."

"I'll take that fifty," Brick said. "Anyone else?"

The others made bets, but Jeff didn't pay any attention. He stood there flat-footed, watching Lanier. The man leaned forward, poked at his head playfully and laughed as Jeff jerked out of his way. Lanier moved in again, but again Jeff ducked, in the same instant bringing up his leg, kicking. The toe of his boot caught the giant in the knee and brought a howl of pain from his throat. He swung wildly but missed, and Jeff countered, smashing his fist against Lanier's crooked nose. Blood smeared from it, streaking around his mouth and over his chin. Jeff used his boot again, finding Lanier's shin, and drove his fist in the giant's face once more. Then he gave ground, ducking, weaving from side to side. Blows showered his shoulders and scraped his head, and finally one got through, smashing him solidly on the forehead.

Jeff was hurled backwards. He lost his balance and fell to the ground. Lanier was rushing him, now, a scream of triumph on his lips. The lashing boot aimed at his head would have ended the fight, too, if it had landed, but Jeff rolled away from it. He jerked to his feet and lunged sideways at Lanier. The drive of his body carried them both down, and they rolled away quickly and got to their feet.

Jeff had hoped, then, for a breathing space, but he didn't get it, because Lanier bulled straight at him. Jeff covered up, backed away, side-stepped, then changed his tactics and charged, forcing the fight. He grazed Lanier's jaw, struck again and hit it squarely. It was like hitting a rock and he decided not to try that again. Instead, he ripped his fists into Lanier's stomach. The man felt it, but showed no signs of weakening.

Lanier jerked a knee up at Jeff's groin and, when he missed, fell against Jeff and locked his arms around him. Jeff could feel them, like tightening steel bands, crushing his ribs. He got his hands up into Lanier's hair and started yanking. That did it. Lanier dropped his arms and swept him aside, then charged in, hammering with his fists.

Jeff went down. A slashing boot scraped the side of his face, setting it afire with pain, and another boot caught him in the ribs. Jeff grabbed it and held on. He reared up, carrying it with him and upsetting Lanier, giving him a chance to use his own boots. His kick pitched Lanier backwards, and the giant rolled away, got up and swung to meet him.

Lanier's face had become a swollen, bloody thing, unrecognizable. He had been badly hurt, but Jeff knew he didn't look much better. Every muscle in his body was shrieking with pain, and the dust they had kicked up was raw in his throat. He could scarcely hold up his arms, and his legs felt shaky. It was hard to focus his eyes. He didn't know how long Lanier could stand it, and, as for himself, he was afraid he was almost through.

Rocking from side to side, he watched Lanier.

Vaguely he heard men shouting, urging Lanier to finish it. Someone shoved him, and then someone stepped up behind him and pushed hard, tilting him off balance. He was thrown squarely into Lanier's swinging fist. He had no chance to duck it or roll with it, and the blow caught him on the side of the jaw. There seemed to be an explosion in his head, scattering every thought, lowering a dark curtain to smother his consciousness. He had no memory of pitching to the ground.

As Brick collected fifty dollars from Doberman, he glanced at Jeff and Paul Lanier. Both of them were down, and Jeff hadn't moved. Lanier might be in better shape, but he didn't look it. He had taken enough punishment to have lost. If he didn't spend a week in bed, it would be surprising.

Doberman followed him when he went outside and said, disgustedly, "I thought you told me Lanier was a fighter."

"You hired him," Brick said. "And he did put up a good battle. You never saw a better fight."

"It didn't take care of Jeff Carmody."

"Why do you say that? Take another look at him. He's damned near dead."

"But now we've got to finish him off."

"Then fix it so it looks right. You don't want to be blamed for Jeff's death. No one around here should be blamed."

Doberman seemed to be thinking about it. "He'll have to disappear," he said finally. "We'll get word around he left the Park. Can't figure anything else."

"I'm going to see Syl," Brick said.

"Why do you have to tell her anything?"

"Damn it, she's no child, Doberman. She knows her brother is here. I'm going to have to tell her something. Fix up a story."

Brick walked on toward the house, taking his time. He didn't look forward to what lay ahead. He wasn't sure what would happen.

He was confused about Syl. He had grown close to her, but there were times when he felt miles away. She wasn't like any other girl he had ever known. She was wholly unpredictable.

When he had figured he was getting some place with her, he had told her a little about his past. This was a good technique; it excited most women to know he had been an outlaw. Of course he made it seem as though he had been a "good" outlaw, driven by circumstances.

Some women accepted what he said, and were thrilled. Some were worried, and wanted to reform him or protect him. Either was fine. Syl, however, hadn't fit into the pattern. She had laughed at him and said, "Of course you're an outlaw. I've known it all the time. And I know why you came here. You want to marry me, because as soon as Grandy dies I'll own half the

Rocking H range. I might fall for it, too. We'll see." Now, what the hell kind of a statement was that?

He went inside, walked back to her room and knocked. She opened the door immediately. She was still dressed, and she looked tense, pale, frightened. She said, "Brick—" but then couldn't say anything more.

"Sit down on the bed," Brick said.

"Is he—dead?"

"No, Syl. Not yet."

"But they mean to kill him."

Brick closed the door and made her sit down. He told her what had happened in the barn, but giving only a brief description of the fight. Then he said, "Syl, I figured it was his only chance. He might weather a fight with Lanier. Anything else—he would have died."

She bit her lips. "How badly is he hurt?"

"I don't know. He's hurt. No question of that."

"Then—what's next?"

He shook his head. He knew pretty well what was next. Just how Jeff would die he wasn't sure, but that was what would happen. Doberman wanted to see him dead.

She leaned forward, "Brick, you've got to help him get away."

"How, Syl?" he asked bluntly. "What chance would I have?"

"You've got to do it."

"I can't, Syl."

She looked at him steadily. "We're finally being honest with each other."

"What do you mean by that?"

"You admitted you came here to make love to me. Then you smiled and said the joke was on you, that you fell in love with your job, that you meant it."

He was scowling now. "I did mean it, Syl. I am in love with you. I didn't mean it to happen, but it did."

"In spite of that, however, what Matt Doberman wants is more important than what I want."

"No."

"It looks that way to me."

He took a brief turn around the room. It suddenly occurred to him that he had never been more confused in his life. Where did he stand today? He didn't know. Where would he stand tomorrow? He had no idea. He glanced at Syl, then stopped pacing and stood staring at her. He had made love to her. She had permitted it. She had even seemed to enjoy it, but what did she think about him, really? Was there any chance in the world that she could fall in love with him? If this was to be a moment of honesty, he was afraid he was lost. He wasn't the kind of a man for Syl. And what kind of life could he give her? At any time he might have to go in hiding, run away.

His old ironic grin settled over his face, and he straightened a little and laughed softly. There was a tight knot in his stomach, but it didn't show on his face. He said, "All right, Syl, I'll help him get away. But will you do something for me?"

"Anything, Brick," she answered quickly.

"Tomorrow, when Doberman finds out I helped Jeff get away, I want to be able to tell him you're going to marry me. You don't have to go through with it. We can stall. But I've got to have an excuse to let Jeff go. If I don't have an excuse, I might not live very long."

She stood up. "Do you really want to marry me?"

"You know I do."

"I want it, too."

Suddenly angry, he walked up to her and put his hands on her shoulders, the fingers digging in until she winced. His voice was harsh. "No, Syl. Not this way. I want you, yes, but not to save Jeff's life. I want you to want nothing but me. It's got to be like that. Just you and me."

"But Brick—"

"No, we've said enough. I've got things to do."

He pushed her away, dropped his hands and swung to the door. There he looked back, and his expression had softened. "Good night, Syl."

One lantern was still burning in the barn. Jeff slowly became aware of it, and for a time it was his only link to reality. Then, gradually, other thoughts came to him, building up a scanty pattern of comprehension. There had been a fight, but how it had ended he didn't remember. It had been a long, hurtful fight. Every muscle in his body was sore, and his face was swollen, burning, caked with blood. His hands were stiff. It was hard to breathe, hard to move, and his head was hammering.

Someone came in and spoke to someone else in the shadows, asking, "How is he? Still out?"

"He's moved a couple times, Brick," the other man said. "Still out, I guess. He took a hell of a beating."

"Lanier took a beating, too," Brick said. "He damn near got whipped. If his brother hadn't shoved him, the fight might have ended differently. What do you think of a man who would do a thing like that?"

"I think it's rotten. Why does Doberman put up with him?"

"He won't, long," Brick said. "I'll take your watch until dawn."

"Doberman said I was to stay here."

"He's changed his mind. He's got a special job for you in the morning. Grab what sleep you can."

The man got up. "I can use it. See you at breakfast."

He left, and after a pause Brick walked over to

where Jeff was lying. He said, "Jeff, you awake?"

"I'm awake," Jeff said thickly.

"I've got a saddled horse tied behind the barn. If I help you that far, do you think you can stick on?"

Jeff was startled. It was Brick who had helped catch him. Why was he letting him go? "I can stick on a horse," he said, but he wasn't at all sure of it.

"If you've got any sense at all, you'll get out of the Park," Brick said.

"You know damned well I won't."

"Then you'll get smashed."

He looked up. "Why are you helping me?"

"For Syl."

Jeff sat up. It wasn't easy. He closed his eyes for a moment against sudden dizziness. Then he looked up again at Brick.

"I know why you're in the Park. I know what you're planning, and I don't like it. You're about as low as a man can get."

"Stow it, Jeff."

"I'll not stow it. I want to talk about it. I'm not going to let you marry my sister."

"Who said I would?" Brick asked shortly.

"It's what you want."

"Yes, that's what I want," Brick admitted. "If I can make it, I will. I'm not sure I can. Anyhow, this isn't the time to talk."

"Give me a gun."

"You couldn't hold one."

Jeff was silent for a moment. Then he asked, "How will Doberman take it when I get away?"

Brick laughed with amusement. "Doberman will explode. He'll rave. He'll yell at me. He'll bite nails, but that's all he can do. You see, I'm important to his plan. I'm needed for Syl. Doberman might want to kill me—but he won't dare."

"Then I'll do it," Jeff said. "I'll ride away. I'll find a gun, then I'll come back."

"Talk to your sister first."

"Why?"

"Because the way this is working out, there are going to be three sides. Your side, Doberman's side—and mine and Syl's. Let's see you stand."

Jeff rolled over on his knees. He got to his feet, but without Brick's help he would have fallen. After a time, however, he could stand alone, and once on a horse he was sure he could stick.

"Try not to make any noise," Brick advised.

Jeff glared at him. "To hell with you, Brick. Watch for me."

They started for the door.

CHAPTER 10

It seemed to take forever to reach his horse. From there, he didn't know where he went, his mind was so clouded by pain. Morning found him in the trees lining the Eden River, less than two hours from the Rocking H. Now he was forced to make a decision. He could set off for Crestline, but it was a long ride. He doubted that he could make it, particularly if Doberman's crowd set off after him. The same was true if he turned to the west, hoping to hide in the hills. Only one other thing seemed possible. He could head for Waldron's; there he might be safe. At the Rocking H Doberman could make his own rules, but if Abe was home it was doubtful that Doberman would get out of line.

Jeff crossed the river, slanting in the direction of the Waldron ranch. Now he began worrying about Vicki and what her attitude toward him would be. For days he had been telling himself he had to see her again. He hadn't really had a chance to talk to her before. Maybe another visit wouldn't help, but he couldn't believe it. They had been close for years. It wasn't right not to try to tear down the wall between them.

The sun was coming up as he rode into the yard, and before he could dismount Abe had come out, recognized him and called a greeting. Then he stared at him again and cried, "Jeff, what the hell's happened? What—"

He didn't finish, but hurried into the yard and came toward Jeff, to steady him as he swung to the ground.

"I had a hard night," Jeff said wryly.

"Who did it?"

"Lanier."

Abe sucked in his breath. "Lanier, huh? It would take six men to handle him. Come on, I'll help you in the house."

"Wait, Abe. They may be after me."

"Doberman?"

"And a few more."

Abe glanced in that direction, his lips tightening. "This is my home. To get inside Doberman would have to walk over me. I don't think he'll try it. Come on."

Mrs. Waldron came out on the porch. She called something to Vicki inside, then joined them in the yard. Vicki appeared at the door, startled, a frightened look on her face.

"We'll take him to Ferd's room," Mrs. Waldron said.

Vicki's head came up. She very nearly said something, but didn't. She turned and went ahead of the others, opening the door to Ferd's room. Inside, she stripped the counterpane from the bed, and Jeff sat down.

"I'll heat more water," Mrs. Waldron said. "Abe, get his boots off. His clothing, too. I'll wash them. Vicki, find one of Ferd's nightshirts in the drawer. Abe's aren't large enough."

Vicki got the nightshirt, and her hands shook as she laid it on the bed. Her voice was strained. "What happened, Jeff?"

"I went to the ranch to see Syl," Jeff answered. "They caught me."

"You didn't try to see Grandy?"

"No."

"Wade said you would try to see his father. He said you meant to make a fight for a share of the ranch."

"No, Vicki."

"Then why did you want to see Syl?"

Abe had finished pulling off his boots. Now he straightened and said, "Vicki, that's enough talking. I'm going to get Jeff out of his clothes."

The girl bit her lips. She turned away but stopped at the door. "Father, what if the Rocking H comes after him?"

"They can ride away again," Abe said gruffly. "Now, scat!"

He had bruises everywhere, but that didn't worry him because he knew they would eventually fade away. More important was the pain in his side; he was afraid he had a broken rib. His hands troubled him, too. His knuckles were barked, swollen, stiff. It might be days before they were normal, and a man without hands was helpless.

Mrs. Waldron did what she could. She cleaned his face, then plastered it with a sticky, oily ointment. She soaked his hands in warm water, to which she had added bichloride of mercury tablets as a guard against infection. Vicki helped, very silent and seemingly worried. She was thin and looked tense and nervous, not at all like the Vicki he had known. She had been a happy person before Ferd's death. He wondered, abruptly, how long it was since she had laughed.

Jeff was still soaking his hands when he heard horses outside. Vicki stepped to the window. She said, "Here they are," and hurried from the room.

"You stay right where you are," Mrs. Waldron said to Jeff. "Keep soaking your hands. Abe knows what to do."

"How many are there?" Jeff asked.

She went to the window. "Mr. Doberman and Wade. Brick Rawson, Bill Traubert and John Creel. And that—Vegas. I'll open the window."

With the window open he could hear what was being said. Doberman was talking. "—and that's the way things stand, Waldron. Jeff came to the ranch and started a fuss. You know Grandy's in bad shape. He can't take a thing like that. We're going to take Jeff to town and throw him in jail."

"But not this morning," Abe said.

"Why not?"

"Jeff's in no shape to go any place, and, if one of your men did it, I'd sign no complaint if I were you. It looks like six men worked him over."

"Then he's faking, Abe. Bring him out."

"Nope."

"Traubert, Creel—go inside and get him."

Suddenly Abe's voice had a brittle edge. "Don't try it. This is my home, Doberman. The first man sets a foot on my porch gets a bullet."

A moment of silence followed. Jeff couldn't see what was happening, but he could imagine it. Abe was in front of his door, just standing there, showing no excitement. Abe never got excited. He was calm, steady and like a rock. Of course he couldn't stand against Doberman's crowd, but, if anyone shot him, the entire Park would be aroused. Doberman probably realized it. He had expected a show of force to be enough. It wasn't.

"So you're setting yourself against the law," he said angrily. "Is that it?"

"Not at all," Abe answered. "What's the law got to do with it. Who gave you a star?"

"Any man can make an arrest."

"Not on my land. On my land I make the decisions. You're trespassing."

Again there was silence. It must have been a bitter moment for Doberman. He spoke once more, half shouting. "By God, Waldron, I won't forget about this." Then he must have wheeled away, for immediately afterward Jeff heard the horses riding away.

Mrs. Waldron left the window, a proud look in her eyes. But she didn't refer to what had happened in the yard. "Keep soaking your hands, Jeff," she ordered. "I'll see about some food."

The Waldrons stayed home most of the day, although Abe did ride away a short distance. When he returned he reported two riders were lurking within sight of the ranch. "I should have taken a shot at them," he said angrily.

"No. Not at all," Jeff answered. "You keep out of it."

Vicki rode out in the middle of the afternoon and was gone two hours. Where she went Jeff didn't know. She may have said something to her parents when she got back, but he was sleeping at the time. He hadn't had a chance to talk to her, either, because she deliberately kept away.

They let him up for supper. By that time he felt much better. He limped a little from the pain in his side, and he was stiff. His face was still badly swollen, but he was stronger. He could use his hands, too, although they felt awkward.

Where Vicki had gone that afternoon was revealed at supper. "I met Wade this afternoon," she announced abruptly.

No one spoke. Jeff stared at his plate. He could

sense that something unpleasant was going to happen.

Vicki spoke again. "Wade told me about last night. One of the men caught Jeff trying to get to Grandy's room. Wade said that he wouldn't have been hurt if he hadn't fought back. He insisted on seeing Grandy."

"No, it didn't happen that way at all," Jeff answered. "I went to see Syl. I was caught as I left her room. They took me to the barn and set Lanier against me. It was a match I couldn't avoid."

"Then either Wade lied, or you are lying," Vicki said.

"Yes. One of us is lying. When you see my sister in town, why not ask her?"

"I intend to."

Abe leaned forward. "Did Wade mention the men watching our ranch?"

"Yes. He said one is Traubert. He has an old quarrel with Jeff. Hoping to avoid trouble, Doberman fired him. If he is watching our ranch, he's doing it on his own."

"And the other man?"

"I don't know about the other man. Neither did Wade."

Abe shook his head wearily. "We're not a family any more, and I don't like it. We're being threatened. When a family is threatened, it needs to stick together. Mother and I took a friend into

137

our home. Our daughter doesn't approve. Let's talk about it."

Vicki's face reddened. "I can't help the way I feel."

"Have you tried?"

"Yes, I've tried. But I know something you don't. Ferd didn't want to ride that outlaw horse. Jeff dared him to do it. That's why I blame him for what happened. Ferd would be living today if Jeff hadn't made him ride the horse."

An angry denial rose in Jeff's throat, but he held it back. This was a time to hold steady. He glanced around the table. "The day before Ferd was killed, we were talking. I told him Grandy had bought some horses, and that we had one no one could ride. I had tried twice, and had been thrown. I said I was going to try again. Ferd asked when, and I told him the next afternoon. He said he'd be there, and, if I couldn't stick on the horse, he'd try it."

Vicki was staring straight at him. "Then what happened the next day?"

"Ferd came by. Syl was home, but inside. Two other men were there, Andy Culp and Syd Wright. Andy is dead. I don't know where Syd is. Wade was there, too. We put a saddle on the horse, and I tried to ride him. I got thrown. Then Ferd said, 'My turn, Jeff.' And I said, 'Go ahead.' Those were our exact words."

"That isn't the way I heard it. You dared Ferd to ride the horse. He didn't want to."

He shook his head wearily. "Vicki, didn't you know your brother at all? He grew up with horses. He's broken many a colt. He was one of the best wranglers in the Park. I thought I was good, too, and to ride an unbroken horse is a challenge. It was to me. It was to Ferd. I didn't dare him. It would have been ridiculous. In fact, I couldn't have stopped him. And why should I? None of us could see the accident ahead."

"I've always said it was an accident," Abe said. "I know how Ferd felt about wrangling, too. Maybe there was a dare, but the dare was from the horse."

Vicki looked at him sharply. "Wade told me— but why would he say such a thing?"

"What kind of a man would talk about his brother, anyhow?" Abe asked.

She didn't answer; her defiance had suddenly collapsed. She covered her face with her hands and began to shake. Jeff searched for something to say to bridge the silence. He wanted to reach out and touch Vicki's arm, but he was afraid she would cringe away. He looked appealingly at Mrs. Waldron.

"Time to soak your hands again," she said briskly, getting to her feet. "Vicki, get the basin. I'll start clearing a place at the table."

They had a quiet night, but the two men watching the ranch hadn't left. Abe found where they had camped for the night—near the corral, where they could keep an eye on the horses. By dawn, they had pulled away, but were still watching from a distance. Abe worked close to the house, Vicki helping him. She had gone to bed early and this morning had said scarcely a word.

"She loved her brother very much," Mrs. Waldron said after they were alone in the house. "When Ferd was killed, she felt she had to blame someone. I think she would have gotten over it, excepting for what Wade told her. Wade fed her anger. He never liked you."

"Not much," Jeff said, and he was putting it lightly.

"I think Vicki is starting to think," Mrs. Waldron continued. "She's proud. She hates to be wrong. She's growing up."

They had a guest for dinner, Dan Hotchkiss. The two men watching the ranch hadn't tried to stop him. Apparently they were only interested in Jeff.

"I came here just to make sure no one steals my hired hand," Dan said, grinning. "Maybe someday I can get him back. Of course, he doesn't look like much."

Jeff laughed. "I can work circles around you. How did you know where I was?"

"The story's all over Crestline."

"What does it sound like?"

"Like this. You rode to the Rocking H and tried to get to your father's room. Paul Lanier was taking care of him. He ordered you not to bother your father, but you wouldn't listen, so Lanier took your gun, roughed you up and dumped you on a horse. The horse wandered here.

"When the sheriff heard about the trouble he offered to put you under arrest, but Doberman wouldn't have it. He said he figured you wouldn't bother them any more. He said you'd had your lesson."

"It was quite a lesson," Jeff said dryly. Then he added his own version.

They sat at the table and talked about it. Abe told Dan of his meeting with the Rocking H riders the morning before and mentioned the two men watching the ranch. "Nothing to worry about now," he said, "but when Jeff's ready to leave I don't know what we'll do."

"We'll work it out," Dan said.

"You're not supposed to be here," Jeff said. "You're supposed to be home with Harriet and the kids."

Dan shrugged. "No rush."

Jeff avoided looking at Vicki. Yesterday she had ridden off to see Wade. Maybe she would see him today. And what would she tell him? It made him sick to feel he couldn't trust her.

"Those hands need another week of treatment," Dan said.

"A week, or even more," Abe said. "Jeff can stay as long as he wishes."

Jeff nodded. "Say a week."

He had been talking chiefly for Vicki's benefit, but after dinner he had a private talk with Dan. He wasn't going to wait a week. It wasn't fair to the Waldrons that he should. His presence kept Abe home. A man doing a range job couldn't stay home. He was leaving tonight.

Dan left, and toward mid-afternoon Vicki left, too. She didn't say where she was going, but Jeff was almost sure it was to meet his brother. It made him bitter, made him want to hit someone. He tried not to think about her.

Before supper, Jeff told Abe what he was going to do but said nothing to the others. Vicki had returned, and tonight she said nothing about where she had been. They played pinochle for a while after supper, and before ten Abe yawned, checked his watch and said it was time for bed.

In half an hour the house was quiet. Jeff, lying on his bed in the darkness, waited impatiently for the minutes to pass. The plan he had set up with Dan was quite simple. Dan was to return to town; then, soon after dark he was to leave, leading an extra horse. He would head for a sharp bend in the river directly south of Waldron's. There he would wait. Jeff would slip from the ranch and walk to the river. It was a three-mile jaunt, but that didn't worry him. His chief problem was getting away from the ranch. The two men on watch were undoubtedly keeping an eye on the corral. If the horses weren't disturbed, they would figure he still was here. It wouldn't occur to them that he would walk.

Abe had given him a gun. Jeff sat up and checked it in the darkness. He wasn't sure how well he could use it, but it was a comforting thing to have it. He stood up, then, and stepped to the door. It creaked as he opened it, but not much, and in a moment he moved on. In another instant, however, he froze, startled at a rustling sound and at a whispered word. "Jeff?"

It was Vicki who had spoken. He recognized her voice almost immediately, and he whirled in the direction of her room. "Yes, Vicki."

She came toward him, a vague, hardly distinguishable figure. "You're leaving! Where? What about the men outside?"

"They're watching the corral," Jeff answered. "I'll be walking. Dan's waiting not too far away. He'll have horses."

He couldn't see her face but could sense she was frowning. "You could have told me, but maybe you didn't trust me. I've wanted a chance to talk to you. It didn't work out that I could. Where are you going, or can you tell me that?"

"I don't know, honestly."

"You're going to stay in the Park?"

"Yes."

"Do you have to?"

"Yes, Vicki."

She suddenly sounded angry. "Then you're going to fight them. You're going to try to get your share of the ranch. It was like Wade said."

"Not exactly like Wade said."

"What else could it be? You're not the Jeff I used to know."

"You're not Vicki."

They stood silent, and to Jeff there seemed to be terrible finality in what they had said. There was a bitter taste in his mouth. His memories of Vicki went back almost as far as he could remember. Something Syl had said to him. How had she put it? *I almost wish we could be children again.* Right now he could better understand what she had meant.

He stirred and looked toward the door. "I'll have to be going, Vicki."

She spoke again. "Then go."

The words had a dead sound. Even the lightest inflection in her voice would have been something to carry with him, to make the moment easier. But it wasn't there. It occurred to him that just now he and Vicki had had their talk. It hadn't taken very long, but perhaps that was good. To stretch it out would have been pointless. He swung toward the door and crossed the room, and from there he looked back. Vicki was probably watching him in the darkness, but he couldn't see her.

In another moment he was outside.

CHAPTER 11

According to Abe, the two men watching the ranch had spent the previous night at a point just west of the corral. Where they were camped tonight he wasn't sure, but undoubtedly they would have followed the same routine and camped where they could watch the horses.

Jeff stood briefly in the deep shadows near the front door, listening, searching the darkness. He couldn't see or hear anything. He edged to the corner in the direction away from the corral, hesitated and then stepped away, moving as silently as he could. This was a tense, critical moment. If they were anywhere near, the two men watching might see him. It was a dark night, but not as dark as it could have been. He took ten steps, twenty, thirty, then stopped abruptly and dropped to the ground. Somewhere off to the left he thought he had heard a rumbling voice.

For a full minute he didn't move. He had turned on his side and was staring in that direction, but he could see nothing. Nor did he hear the voice again. Finally he got up on his knees, still muscle-tight, breathless. Then he caught it again, low, almost indistinguishable, but certainly a man's voice.

Once more he dropped to the ground. He hadn't

blundered straight into the two men watching the horses, but he had come very close to it. They were somewhere off to the south, maybe a stone's throw from where he was. If they had looked this way, they might have seen him.

Jeff took another minute to steady himself; then, switching directions, he turned north, crawling, hugging the ground. He didn't get up until he was sure he was safe. Then, in turning toward the river, he made a wide circle to the east. From there, it was merely a matter of walking quietly.

Because he had had to cover more ground than he had expected and had been delayed near the house, he didn't reach the river until after midnight. He knew Dan would have been worrying, but when he got to the bend no one was in sight.

Still under the trees, he ventured a call. "Dan! Dan, where are you?"

A figure came in sight. "Over here, Jeff."

The voice startled him. It wasn't Dan who had answered. It sounded like a woman—like Gwen. Damn it, what was Gwen doing here?

He hurried toward her and spoke gruffly. "What are you doing here? Where's Dan?"

"I took his place."

"Why?"

"Two reasons, Jeff. First, I wanted to. Second, it was safer. Dan didn't have an extra horse in town. If he borrowed one from Will Shackle, someone might find out. Mother and I each have a horse. They won't be missed."

"You could have loaned Dan a horse."

She laughed easily. "You weren't supposed to figure that out. Anyhow, if Dan hadn't gone home, Harriet would have worried. He said you'd be here before midnight. Did you have trouble?"

He shook his head, studying her. She was tall and slender, and she had a nice figure, a boyish figure, in the jeans she was wearing. Perhaps she didn't have Vicki's beauty, but no one would ever say she was plain.

"How's Vicki?" she asked suddenly.

He shrugged. "Vicki's all right."

"That doesn't tell me much."

The way she said it made him laugh, the first real laugh he had had for several days. He expected her to join in, but she didn't, and after a minute he asked, "What's the matter?"

"I don't think it's funny."

"Maybe it isn't, but I couldn't help laughing. Should I kiss you?"

"No." The answer was emphatic, and she stepped back, half raising her arms to repel him if he stepped forward.

"Why?" Jeff asked bluntly. "You kissed me in the restaurant. It was a good kiss, too."

"I know just how good it was," Gwen said. "But this is serious to me. Maybe we better ride. The horses are tied back in the trees."

She was angry, sharply angry. He could feel it in her voice, could sense it in her attitude. He had said the wrong thing, but, damn it, she was too sensitive. "Wait a minute, Gwen," he said, suddenly weary. "We'll get to the horses, but don't jump me tonight. I'm not up to it."

Her head came up. "Why? What happened?"

"I don't want to talk about it."

She was silent for a moment, staring at him. What she could see in his swollen face he couldn't imagine. But some of the strain that had gripped her faded, and when she spoke her voice was softer. "If we stay, I'm going to have to ask questions. So maybe we'd better ride."

They headed east in the direction of Crestline, and after a while they started talking. Jeff explained his trip to the Rocking H to see Syl. He told her how he had been caught, of the fight with Lanier and how he had escaped. "Pretty soon," he said, grumbling, "you'll know everything I know."

"That's what I want," Gwen said, smiling.

"A hold on me, huh?"

"It's supposed to be nice—but tell me more about Syl."

He did, and they talked about her for a while. It seemed to him that Syl was the key person in the entire situation, and Gwen agreed, although she wasn't sure what to do next.

"How soon will she do something final, one way or the other?" she asked slowly.

"I don't know. They'll hurry her all they can. If Brick and Syl get married, Doberman's over the first hump. And the biggest. They'll wait for Grandy to die. Wade will be next."

"I wish you could have seen Grandy."

"I didn't have the chance—and maybe it's just as well. Syl says he's terribly weak. She said another thing. She said Grandy hadn't given up—that he still thinks that someday he'll be able to get out of bed."

"Is there any chance at all?"

"No, I'm afraid not. But Grandy's like that. He's been stubborn all his life, and he'll be stubborn about dying. It'll be a battle to the end."

Gwen smiled. "There's something immortal about people like Grandy. They die, I know, but they never seem to die. They live on in the courage of others. But what about you, Jeff? Where do you fit in? What are you fighting about?"

Jeff tried to put in words just how he felt. "It's not a share of the range that I want," he said slowly. "If Grandy wanted to cut me out, that's all right. But it doesn't change the past. Grandy and Syl, and even Wade, are my family. The danger that threatens them threatens me. A man named Doberman has moved in and taken our home. That's not easy to take."

"What if Syl marries Brick?"

"I can't believe she wants it."

"Are you sure, Jeff? Love's a funny thing. You can't control it. It gets off the trail. It isn't always logical. It doesn't always behave the way you think it should. It can make you happy even when you're miserable. I know what I'm talking about, and don't laugh."

Jeff decided they had been serious long enough. He raised his hands in mock surrender. "No more laughing."

She suddenly smiled. "You'll laugh again. Where are you going tonight?"

"Who knows?"

"Do you want to hide?"

"I want to stall. I want Syl to have more time to think; then I'll want to see her again. I want my hands to get better. Yes, I need a place to hide for a week."

"Want a suggestion?"

"Go ahead."

"How about our place? I mean the ranch we used to own before Daddy died. The man who took it couldn't make a go of it, and we had to take it back. The bank is trying to sell it but hasn't been able to. The buildings are just sitting there, empty."

Jeff thought about it, nodding. It would be ideal. It was back in the hills, out of the way, and across the Park from the Rocking H. It might be a week or longer before anyone might think of looking for him there. And it would be more comfortable than living outside.

"I'd need groceries," he said.

"I could bring some tomorrow night."

"Who would cook for me?" He was grinning. "Who would take care of me?"

Her eyes flashed dangerously. "Don't think I couldn't. But you're not ready, Jeff. When I start a thing like that, it'll go on. I'm like that."

"Something to think about, huh?"

"Yes. Something to think about. But, if you're going to our place in the hills, you ought to cut off here."

"I ought to see you home, Gwen."

"Why? I got here alone, didn't I? I'm a competent person. See you tomorrow night."

"Tomorrow night, Gwen."

She waved, wheeled away and rode on. Jeff watched her until she was out of sight.

It was several miles from the eastern edge of the Park to the high walls of the Cimarron range. The intervening space was hilly and well-timbered, but here and there were meadow areas. When the Sennetts had moved there, no one had objected. It was free land, and not very valuable. While they were living there the Sennetts hadn't built up much of a ranch. Frank Sennett had never run many cattle; in the main, they lived on the land. What he could make on his cattle had supplied his other needs and provided a small margin of profit.

The buildings were still in good condition; Frank had built them to stand. The main house was bone dry inside, and some of the furniture was still here. The stove drew nicely, and the beds were comfortable. Jeff stabled his horse, then slept most of the next day. In the late afternoon he took care of his horse, then gathered wood, cleaned the pans and swept out the place. He was getting hungry by then, but he didn't expect Gwen until late, so he sat on the porch and watched the sun go down.

He had time to do some thinking, now, and he had a wide range of things to think about. But, for some reason or other, Gwen was more on his mind than anything else. He would see her soon and he was anxiously waiting—and not only because of the groceries she would bring. He wanted to take another good look at her. Of course, since she and her mother had moved to town, he had seen her every time he went there and had talked to her a number of times. He knew a little about her. He had thought about her as a friend, but a few days ago she had moved into his life much more importantly. Without much question she was in love with him. If this went on, soon he wouldn't be able to dislodge her. She would be there always—which might not be a bad idea.

Jeff scrubbed his bristling jaw. A man thinking about a girl didn't have any business wearing a beard. He hoped Gwen would bring a razor.

She came in sight suddenly, turning from a fold in the hills across a narrow meadow. Jeff waved, then stepped out in the yard and stood waiting. Behind her to the west, the light, low clouds had taken on the sunset colors of the evening. A gentle breeze sifted through the hills, cooling the heat of the day. In a tree near the house, two jays were chattering at each other, or at him. Something stirred through Jeff's blood, sharpening his perceptions. He watched as she came closer, sure she would be smiling. She was.

"Hungry?" she asked as she reined up.

"Like a bear."

She swung lightly to the ground, before he could help her. "Then I'll take the stuff inside and start supper. You can take care of my horse. But don't unsaddle him. I can't stay long."

"Why not?"

She took his breath away. "Jeff, I'd like to stay all night—and every night. Some day I may. You'd better be awfully careful. Now, take care of my horse."

He stepped toward her. "Gwen—"

She backed away, laughing and shaking her head. "No, Jeff. Supper comes first. I mean it."

Supper came first. Then what? He stood staring at her.

"I shouldn't have said that," Gwen stated. "I don't want to make it a game. Let's start again. Hello, Jeff."

"Hello, Gwen," he said, frowning.

"Suppose you take care of my horse while I start supper. Please, Jeff."

He managed to grin.

She had brought two sacks of supplies. He carried these inside for her, then took care of her horse. By the time he had finished, she had started supper.

"What can I do to help?" he asked from the door.

"Nothing here," Gwen said. "But you might shave. I brought a razor. It's on the table. I'm not sure it'll shave your whiskers, but you could try."

Jeff found the razor. "Some women don't mind a beard," he said.

"But I do."

"Then off they go," Jeff said.

They had supper by lamplight and it was a pleasant meal. The talk was light. At times it bordered on their relationship, but when it did Gwen steered it in another direction. After they had eaten, Jeff helped with the dishes. Then they blew out the lamp and went outside. It was a dark, quiet night.

"Now we'll talk," Jeff said.

But Gwen shook her head. "Not long, for I can't

stay. I told you that. I'll be tired from the ride, and I have to get up early. My mother took the supper alone tonight. I want to be on the job for breakfast. I'm going right away."

He didn't want her to go like this, and he took her arm. "Stay just a few minutes."

"I can't. I'm afraid."

"That's ridiculous."

"No, it isn't. I'm what they call a brazen hussy. I say what I think. You told me to go after the man I wanted, and I've tried. It's a little wearing, so I don't dare to stay. Before I leave, however, I want to leave something behind. It's this."

She swung toward him and into his arms, lifting her face to be kissed. Jeff had been startled in the restaurant, but tonight he was ready. He pulled her tight, his arms locked behind her back. He could feel her warmth and the soft, hard pressure of her body. Her lips were moist, sweet and sharply alive under his. When she started to push him away, he didn't want to let her go.

"You can't go now," he whispered.

"But I have to."

She broke away, and something warned him to let her go. They walked into the yard, to the place where he had tied her horse. A moment later she was in the saddle.

"I'd like to ride with you," Jeff said. "But it wouldn't be wise. Will you come again?"

"No, Jeff."

"Why?"

Her hands were folded on the saddle horn. He couldn't see her face clearly, but he thought she was frowning. She said, "Jeff, I want you. I want you so badly it hurts. But that's not enough. You've got to do some wanting on your own— and mean it. There'll be no more samples like tonight. If it ever happens again, I won't stop. I wouldn't be able to."

He stretched his hand toward her. "Gwen—"

But she didn't wait for him. Wheeling away, she disappeared in the darkness. In another minute, even the hoofbeats of her horse were gone.

CHAPTER 12

Bill Traubert was on the defensive. He explained how Jeff Carmody had escaped, and he claimed that he and Creel, alone, couldn't possibly have prevented it. Two men hadn't been enough to cover the ranch. What had happened wasn't his fault.

"Then the fault is yours," Doberman said, swinging to face Brick Rawson.

"Why me?" Brick asked mildly.

"We had our hands on Jeff right here. You were the one who let him go."

Brick shrugged. "I still think it was wise. It wouldn't have looked right if Jeff had been killed here. Why are you worried, anyhow? He's in no shape to fight back. He's been disowned by Grandy, anyhow."

Doberman paced his cabin angrily. He knew that what Brick had said was true, but only if you looked on the surface. He was looking deeper. Jeff would be a real threat to some of the things he wanted to do in the future. He had always been well-liked in the Park, and that ugly story they had started of what Jeff had done in Denver hadn't done anything to hurt his popularity. If he stayed here and asked the wrong questions, he could be damned annoying.

"Get a night's sleep, Traubert," he said abruptly. "Then head for town. I told the sheriff I was going to fire you. Spread the news. You don't work here any more."

"Then what?"

"You got a grudge against Jeff, haven't you?"

"I really got one now." Traubert grinned. "Missed some sleep the last two nights."

"Then get him. Maybe he went to Dan Hotchkiss's. If he ain't there, wait in town. Jeff's bound to hit town pretty soon."

"When do I get paid?"

"After the job. Now, clear out. Not you, Brick. Something I want to talk to you about."

The others who had been present left. Brick closed the door, then stood against it. He didn't seem worried about a thing, but then he never did.

"Where's Syl?" Doberman asked.

"In her room, I guess."

"Where did you go tonight?"

"Just took a short ride. She was tired."

"Nothing wrong?"

"Nope. Not a thing."

Doberman's eyes had narrowed, and he stared at Brick sharply. "I talked to her today. I asked her how soon you two meant to get married. She stalled."

"We haven't set the date."

"Set it."

Brick's voice showed a trace of irritation. "You're pushing me, Doberman. I don't like it. I'll marry the girl. I'll get my hands on her land, but lay off. Let me do it my way."

"I want you to set the date," Doberman said. "Now, get the hell out of my sight."

Brick grinned provokingly. "Sure. Glad to."

After the man had left, Doberman continued to pace the floor. Brick Rawson worried him. In the first place, Brick had come here with Jeff, and that still troubled him. Then, definitely, Brick had set Jeff free the other night. He had a reason, maybe a good reason, but he still didn't like it. Brick, he decided, was a man to watch.

He left the cabin, walked to the house and went back to Grandy's room. On the way he listened at Syl's door, but he could hear nothing.

In Grandy's room he lit the lamp, closed the door and walked up to the bed. Grandy lay motionless on his back, his eyes closed. He looked the same as every day, the pallor of death in his skin.

"Wake up, old man," Doberman said. "I want to talk to you."

Grandy didn't move, didn't open his eyes.

Doberman leaned over and shook him. "Wake up, old man."

Grandy looked up. "You here again?"

"Why not, old man? Sure I'm here again. Why don't you die?"

"I have to kill you first."

Doberman laughed harshly. He was going to miss these little sessions when Grandy died. He said, "Old man, your daughter's going to marry a man who works for me. It's all set up."

"Where's my son?"

"Losing money in a poker game in the bunk-house."

"I mean my other son."

"You don't have any other son. If you're thinking of Jeff, he's probably dead."

Grandy shook his head. "If he was dead, you'd boast of it."

Doberman was irritated. He said, "Old man, you don't have much time. I want to see Syl and Brick married; then Wade's going to have an accident. After that, you can leave us."

Grandy said nothing. He closed his eyes again.

Doberman stared down at him, then shrugged and blew out the lamp. He walked to the door and opened it, then spoke in a low voice. "Good night, old man. Hang on for a few more days. I'll bring you a piece of the wedding cake."

He was laughing as he walked up the corridor.

Jeff spent the next five days at the old Sennett ranch. He snared rabbits for fresh meat and made a number of exploring trips toward the Cimarrons. Near the ranch he killed seven rattlesnakes. As near as he could tell, no riders had come near the place. The swellings on his face had gone down, and the pain in his side had almost disappeared. His hands were better. The scabs on his knuckles were constantly breaking, but the soreness had lessened.

On the sixth day he left, swinging south, then circling toward the Hotchkiss place. He got there late in the afternoon, and Harriet and the children seemed glad to see him.

"But we've worried about you," she told him. "Of course we had it on good authority that you were safe. Did you see anyone riding in?"

"Not a soul," Jeff answered.

"Then maybe he's gone."

"Who?"

"Bill Traubert. For two days he haunted the range. Dan saw him several times, but he didn't come close."

Dan himself rode in a few minutes later. "Ready to go back to work?"

"Not right away." Jeff grinned.

"That's what I was afraid of."

Supper wouldn't be ready for half an hour, giving them time to talk while they cared for their horses. "I'll want to borrow one in the morning," Jeff said. "I don't want to go back to town on one of Gwen's horses."

"Then pick the one you want," Dan said. "Are you sure you want to go to town."

"Any reason I shouldn't?"

"Traubert. They say Doberman fired him, but he's been hanging around. Was out here looking for you. Maybe he left the Park, but he might be in town."

Jeff shook his head thoughtfully. He said, "Dan, I don't want to run into Traubert. It wouldn't gain a thing, but I can't spend the rest of my life hiding from him, either. I want to go to town. If Traubert's there, I'll have to chance it."

"They say he's fast, Jeff."

"Every gunslinger thinks he's fast. Have you seen Gwen?"

"Saw her the day after she took your groceries. She should have looked tired, but she didn't. Don't ever worry about Gwen."

"What's happened at the Rocking H?"

"Nothing new. Grandy's living. It's amazing the way he hangs on."

"Heard anything from Syl?"

"They're talking about her and Brick. Most people don't like it."

"Wade?"

"Same as usual."

Nothing startling had happened, which was an encouraging sign. They turned toward the house. "I'll be leaving before you get up in the morning," Jeff said. "I want to hit town early. That way, I may not run into trouble."

"Have to go in tomorrow, myself," Dan said.

Jeff grinned and shook his head. "No, you won't, Dan, and I'll say the same thing to Harriet. Last time I was walking into a trap, but tomorrow no one knows I'm coming. When I really need help, I'll let you know."

He left before dawn, and by nine he was in Crestline, tying his horse at the rail in front of Bennett's Restaurant. It was late for the breakfast hour, and the room was empty when he entered. This was more luck that he had expected. The restaurant, as much as the saloon, was a gathering place, seldom vacant.

A bell had tinkled on the door when he entered, but he was at one of the side tables before Gwen came in from the kitchen. She saw him instantly and stopped. Her face colored, and she caught her breath.

Jeff grinned. "Good morning, Gwen."

It took her only a moment to regain her composure; then she walked around the counter and came toward him. "Good morning, Jeff. Coffee or breakfast?"

He was enjoying himself. "Is that all you have to say?"

"What do you expect?"

"How would it be if I reached for you?"

He eyes flashed a warning, but she was laughing. "Don't try it. If I shout for Mother he'll come from the kitchen with a pan of hot

163

water. Once she did. You should have seen what happened. I've a message for you."

"From whom?"

"Your sister, Syl. She wants to see you. Do you know a place called the Cave of Adullam?"

The cave had been one of their childhood rendezvous. It was north and west of the ranch, but in a wooded area, well-hidden. He could get there safely. Still looking up at Gwen, he nodded.

"She said she'd check there, every day starting today. I said I might see you in a day or two."

"Thanks, Gwen."

"I asked her about Brick, too. She's in love with him."

Jeff was scowling, now. He was afraid Gwen was right. So where did that leave him? What should he do?

"I have another message for you," Gwen said. "I don't want to give it to you."

"Why?"

"I just don't want to. But I will. Vicki wants to see you."

His heart jumped. He couldn't help it. What did Vicki want? When he saw her last he had thought they would never speak again, but maybe he was wrong. Maybe she had been thinking.

"Coffee or breakfast?" Gwen asked, and her voice sounded flat.

He stared at her, and the forbidding expression on her face was unmistakable. He could understand the reason, too. She had seen his interest in Vicki's message; he hadn't been able to hide it. He was suddenly angry with himself. He said, "Gwen, you've got to—"

"Coffee or breakfast?" she interrupted.

"Breakfast. And Gwen—"

He suddenly didn't know what to say. Back there in the hills he had thought he knew how he felt. All week he had been looking forward to the time when he could see Gwen again. He had thought that when he got here there would be nothing left between him and Vicki. But he was wrong. Vicki was still there. He didn't want to admit it, but there it was.

"I'll get your breakfast," Gwen said.

She hurried away, and Jeff watched her, shifting uneasily. Someone else came in. Sheriff McEllis. Jeff glanced over that way, scowling. Damn it, why did the sheriff have to come in right now? He wanted to see Gwen again.

The sheriff came over to his table, pulled out a chair and sat down. He said, "Morning, Jeff."

"Good morning, Sheriff."

"Where you been?"

"Resting."

"That's no answer, but we'll let it ride. What was the idea of kicking up a fuss out at the Rocking H? Grandy's a mighty sick man."

Jeff wanted to avoid an argument with the sheriff, but he was afraid it was going to be hard. Since their relationship was already strained, almost anything he said was going to sound wrong. He tried to jump over the problem. "Sheriff, I'm sorry about what happened, but there's not much point in talking about it, is there?"

"Maybe so, maybe not," the sheriff answered. "I should have thrown you in jail for what you did, but Doberman said to forget it. I'm not that soft."

It was amusing to think that Doberman was soft, but Jeff made no comment. Gwen came with his breakfast, and didn't look at him when she served him. Two other men came in and took another table. She took them coffee, then brought a cup to the sheriff.

"I want to tell you something," the sheriff was saying. "From now on, you're to keep away from the Rocking H. That's an order. Understand?"

"Sure I understand," Jeff said easily.

"One more thing," the sheriff continued. "Doberman's been helpful. He's tried to prevent any trouble in the Park. Just because of the feeling between you and Bill Traubert, he fired Traubert and told him to get out of the Park. I suppose he will in a day or so, but he hasn't gone yet. He's still hanging around town."

"I haven't got anything against Traubert," Jeff said.

"That isn't the way he puts it. He says he's still after you. I warned him I'd stand for no gun-fight. I'm saying the same thing to you. If you run into each other and there's any shooting, whoever can walk away goes to jail."

"I won't start anything," Jeff said.

It was a sobering thing, however, to realize that Traubert was in town. His presence meant imminent danger. If Jeff stayed in town very long, it would be impossible to avoid him. Another thought ran through his mind. Doberman was more clever than he had realized. He had said he had fired Traubert. Now, if they met and there was any trouble, Doberman was in the clear. He had seemed to be trying to avoid it.

The sheriff got to his feet. "I'll be watching you, Jeff," he said heavily.

"Watch Traubert," Jeff said, grinning.

Gwen brought him fresh coffee; then she stood at the table, frowning. "Let me see your hands."

He held them out. "Don't worry about my hands."

"But if you meet Bill Traubert—"

"Don't even think about it."

She sat down suddenly. "I can't think of anything else. In a minute you'll go out on the street. I don't want you to go. I want you to stay here."

"I thought you were angry, Gwen."

She shook her head. "I wasn't angry. I felt hurt. Maybe I expected too much, but I don't want to talk about it."

She looked shaky, and she glanced over her shoulder at the door. Her hands were on the table, and Jeff reached over to cover them with his own. He said, "Steady, Gwen. We have to take a few chances. If the cave men had stayed in their holes, we'd still be living as they did."

She tried to smile. "I wish we had a cave, right here. I thought I was brave. I'm afraid I'm not."

"But I told you not to worry," Jeff said. "My horse is right in front. When I leave here I'm going to swing into the saddle and ride out. In a minute, I'll be gone. And Gwen—I'll be back."

"I want you to come back."

He patted her hands, then stood up and walked to the door. There, he tested the gun in his holster, to make sure it was loose. Gwen would notice that, he knew, but it couldn't be helped. And it didn't mean anything in particular; it was simply a precautionary measure. There wasn't much chance of running into Traubert if he left town.

He looked back at Gwen and waved, then stepped outside. Up the street the sheriff was standing in front of his office. Nearer, Hap Ibberton was sweeping his saloon porch, and across from him a woman was entering the Boston Store. Three men were in front of the bank, one of them Doc Hymen, and walking toward them was Pops Jelbert. Jeff noticed all this in a sweeping glance. He stepped to the tie rail and was loosening the reins when he heard Traubert's sharp, high voice coming from behind him, at the corner of the restaurant. "Turn around, Carmody!"

He swung slowly, dropping his hand close to his gun. His body had tightened up. He had been prepared for this, but hadn't really expected it. He stared at Traubert sharply. Traubert was standing partially crouched, his right hand hovering above his gun, his face in a grimace.

"You can't run this time," Traubert said. "Go for your gun, anytime."

"Why?" Jeff asked quietly.

"You know why. Grab your gun."

Jeff managed a smile, even as he realized a man in his position wasn't supposed to smile. And he stood waiting—let Traubert make the first motion, stretch out the tension between them. He had a good reason for it. A thing like this took rocklike nerves. The weight of every second was like a pound. Let it mount up. He could take it, because he wasn't anxious to use his gun. But how long could Traubert take it?

He watched the man closely and saw faint perspiration on his forehead. It hadn't been there a moment before. And his eyes had changed. He didn't look as confident now.

A noise rumbled up through Jeff's throat. It was supposed to be a laugh, and perhaps it sounded like that to Traubert. It was enough. A hoarse cry erupted from Traubert's throat. "Now, Carmody! Now!"

He clawed at his holster, whipping up his gun. Jeff's arm moved at the same moment, and he heard the explosion of his shot and, in its echo, Traubert's. Something scraped his thigh like the sting of a whip. He fired again, but he probably hadn't needed to. Traubert was rearing backwards. He hit the corner of the building, dropped his gun and twisted sideways, pitching to the ground. He didn't move again.

For a breathless second Jeff didn't move; then he holstered his gun and wiped his other hand across his face. It came away soaking wet, and his legs suddenly felt weak. Gwen appeared abruptly at the restaurant door. She was pale, wide-eyed, and her hands were clutched at her breast.

"It's all right, Gwen," Jeff said thickly. "Couldn't be helped. I wish—"

He didn't finish what he was saying. Up the street he caught a glimpse of Art McEllis. The sheriff was hurrying toward him, and he remembered what he had promised. The way this had happened, any court in the land would have set him free. It was a clear case of self-defense. But the sheriff could put him in jail for a while if he wanted to, and he probably did. And that was something Jeff didn't want.

His horse had danced into the street, the reins trailing. Jeff twisted that way, caught the horse and swung into the saddle. By this time the sheriff was running, shouting at him.

"Can't stop now," Jeff called back. "See you later."

He wheeled down the street, lifting his horse to a gallop, then looked over his shoulder. A crowd was gathering at the restaurant, but out in front, in the street, Gwen was waving. The sheriff was waving, too, but his fist was clenched.

CHAPTER 13

The headwaters of Latigo Creek were high in the hills to the west. Where it ran into the Park it took a parallel course to the Eden, but Sentinel Hill came in the way, and there Latigo Creek slanted to the north, eventually joining the Eden. On its way it picked up the waters of a number of small unnamed streams. One started from a trickling spring rising in a hilly, wooded area north of the Rocking H. Jeff had found it while stalking an imaginary Indian when he was about twelve. Several years later, when Syl, Wade and he had been out riding, they had been caught in a heavy rain, and he had steered them to a cave near the spring. At the time, Syl had been nine and Wade had been ten.

It was Syl who had named the place the Cave of Adullam. She had picked up the name from reading the Bible. The Cave of Adullam, she had explained, had been a hiding place for David.

"Who was David?" Wade had asked.

"He was the king," Syl had explained inaccurately. "A wicked man named Saul took his place, and David had to flee for his life. But he found a cave where he was safe. He called it the Cave of Adullam."

"I don't think much of your David," Wade had

said. "If he was the king, why didn't he kill his enemies? That's what I would have done."

"The Lord had set his face against him," Syl had said. "But after he changed, he vanquished his enemies. After that, he could leave the cave."

But Wade hadn't been impressed. "I'd never flee to a cave."

"You did today," Syl had said. "You fled from the rain."

Wade hadn't cared for the cave, but Syl had loved it. Or perhaps she had fallen in love with the idea of a place that could be hers. For several years it had been one of her favorite retreats, and she had made it into a playhouse. They had had a reasonable amount of freedom, and the cave was within five miles of the ranch. She could get there in a few minutes by horseback, and Grandy had inspected it and said it was safe.

It was pleasant to recall those days. Those had been times when he and Syl and Wade got along quite well. They quarreled sometimes, but that was natural and unimportant, and if Wade and Syl joined against him it hadn't worried him. They had a closer blood tie, and were closer in years. Later, unfortunately, it had made a difference. By the time Wade was fourteen or fifteen he had begun to worry about his position at the ranch. He was his father's only real son. He had begun to think that Jeff was in the way.

Six or seven miles above Crestline, Jeff left the

road and swung west. By late afternoon he was north of Waldron's. He could have dropped in for supper quite easily, and he was tempted to do it. Vicki wanted to see him. That gave him a good excuse.

He had a cigarette, puzzling over what she wanted. He felt a need to see her, but something held him back. It occurred to him then that he was afraid of what she might say. But that was ridiculous—why should he be afraid? He pinched out the fire of his cigarette, dropped it and stared bleakly in the direction of the Waldron ranch. Then, abruptly, he rode on west. He would see Vicki, of course, but it was more important to see his sister. That came first.

It was near midnight before he reached the Cave of Adullam. Syl wasn't there, but he hadn't expected her. She probably would come in the morning. He found a place to camp, and soon he was asleep.

Syl arrived by ten. She rode into the clearing at the spring, then looked up at the cave above. She looked tired and thinner, but she was smiling. The cave probably held good memories.

Jeff waited, listening to see whether anyone was following. When he was fairly sure she was alone, he stepped into sight, calling, "Good morning, Syl."

She turned quickly toward him. "Jeff. I wasn't sure—"

"That I'd remember the cave?"

"No. I wasn't sure you'd get my message. I wasn't even sure you'd come."

"Why not?"

"The last time you went to see me wasn't very pleasant."

"But that wasn't your fault."

She swung to the ground. "They say Paul Lanier once killed a man with his fists. He's like—he's like a beast."

He took the reins of her horse and tied it near by. Then they found a place to sit above the spring. "You're sure you weren't followed?" Jeff asked.

She shook her head, smiling. "I won't be followed. Most of the men are away, but, if anyone followed me, he'll have to answer to Brick. That's one advantage of having a man. He's a protection."

"Where is he now, Syl?"

"Home. He knows where I've gone, and why. If you agree, I want to bring him back this afternoon."

Jeff frowned. "We'll see about it."

They sat silently there in the shade for a while. Syl glanced up at the cave again. "I climbed there the other day. It's just the same, but it seems smaller."

"We're bigger."

"And older, Jeff. I feel very old. But I'm young,

too. You're not going to like what I have to say."

"I might, Syl."

"No. You won't. I know what I want, but I'm trying to bargain. This is what I want. I want Brick. But, in addition, I want you and Wade unharmed and home again. And I want Matt Doberman and all the men he's hired kicked out of the Park."

He laughed, not really amazed at what she had said.

"That's a tall order."

"But that's what I want."

"What does Brick say?"

"He says we can try it—but what will happen he can't promise."

"Are you really in love with him?"

"Yes."

"What about him?"

She looked him straight in the eye. "Jeff, I honestly think he loves me."

"So what will happen?"

"Jeff, I don't know. I'm going to marry Brick. After Grandy's death, I'll own a share of the range. Matt Doberman wants it all. He thinks he'll get it through Brick, but Brick isn't the kind to hand it over for nothing. It's inevitable that they'll clash."

"And maybe I can help him?" Jeff asked dryly.

She looked up sharply. "Why not? A share should be yours."

"Grandy didn't think so."

"When he made his new will he was angry, and sick. He didn't mean it."

Jeff leaned back on his elbows. "How is he, Syl?"

"Weaker, I suppose. I went to see him late last night. He woke up. I sat down and told him about Brick—and me. Then I talked about you, and Wade, and Matt Doberman. I told him everything. Then I lied. I said we had a plan to work things out, that he wasn't to worry. I don't know how much he heard, because halfway through he went to sleep. Or seemed to."

"Then he must be sick. You shouldn't have talked to him."

"I just—felt I had to."

"How's Wade?"

"Jeff, what are we going to do about him? He's getting worse. He had a fight with Doberman the other day. He acted like a little king. Brick says if he'd acted that way with Vegas, Vegas would have killed him."

"We may not be able to save him," Jeff said gruffly.

"We've got to."

He shook his head, sitting up again. "Let's be honest, Syl. We're not playing games. If a clash is inevitable between Brick and Doberman, Brick might be killed. If I get in it, I may die, too. Or even you."

"What if Brick and I left? What if we ran away?"

"I don't think he would. Then, what about Wade? He wouldn't have the sense to run. He feels like he's on the top of the heap. He loves it."

"Then—what if I didn't get married?"

"I don't know what they'd do then. Something. They're in control."

She took a deep breath. "You mean—there's no easy way out?"

"That's it, Syl."

"Can I bring Brick to see you?"

He nodded slowly. "Why not, Syl? I'd like to see him. The guy interests me. Maybe he's worse than Doberman."

For some reason she didn't get angry. Instead she laughed, shaking her head. "You just don't know him, Jeff. I know everything you can say against him, but beyond that he's kind and he has a tenderness he hides. I've spent hours with him. I know how he thinks. I've seen under the shell he wears, and I like what's there."

"You've got it bad," Jeff said, grinning.

"Yes, I have."

"If you get married, when would you do it?"

"Next Sunday. That's in four days. There's a notice in town that the circuit preacher will be here Sunday."

Her cheeks were pink. She was looking up at the sky, and her eyes had softened and the lines in her face had disappeared. Damned if she didn't look like a bride. He reached abruptly for her hands and squeezed them. "Syl, all the luck in the world. If Brick doesn't treat you right, I'll beat him. Now, go get him."

Syl was laughing as she rode away. Jeff was glad she could, but he wasn't sure how long she could keep it up. He was skeptical about Brick, uncertain of her future. She had fallen in love, but under a tension that colored everything about her. Marriage was a long pull. It was filled with routines, with day-by-day tasks that were unexciting. It could become monotonous. He couldn't see how well Brick would fit into a thing like that.

He had a cold dinner, then waited as patiently as he could. The afternoon was half gone before he heard them. They rode into the clearing, Syl leading the way and Brick following, and as they got there Syl looked back and said something, laughing. Brick answered her, grinning; then he swung to the ground and lifted her down. He didn't seem worried about a thing.

It was Syl who saw him first, and she called, "Well, here he is, Jeff."

He walked toward them. "Hello, Syl. Hello, Brick."

Brick half raised his arm. "Howdy, Jeff."

Then they stood there, measuring each other. Jeff couldn't help feeling antagonistic, and he was sure Brick probably felt the same way.

Syl stamped her foot. "Stop glaring, both of you."

"I wasn't glaring," Jeff said.

"Me neither," Brick said.

He stepped forward and put out his hand, and Jeff took it.

"That's more like it," Syl said. "Now we'll talk."

Brick took care of the horses, and then they found a place to sit. Without wasting any time at all, Brick jumped into the middle of the problem. "Jeff, we've been thinking of getting married Sunday."

Jeff nodded. "Syl told me."

"You don't sound glad."

Jeff looked straight at him. "I just hope she isn't making a mistake."

"She could do better," Brick replied, and he was frowning. "There's no reason not to be honest. I came here to marry her. It was a part of Doberman's plan. He wrote me about this place. He said the old man was dying, that there was a daughter and two sons. He said one of the sons was a fool who could easily get killed. The other son was away, but wouldn't get back. That left the daughter. She was marriageable, pretty. Maybe I could get her. If I couldn't, they'd try something else."

"You ought to be damned proud," Jeff snapped.

"Now don't get me riled," Brick said angrily. "That was the way it was set up. I didn't do it. It was Doberman's plan. I came here, sure, but I didn't know what I was going to do when I got here. I had a dull job. This looked interesting, so I came to take a look. What was wrong with that?"

"You're marrying the girl."

"I fell in love with her."

"Maybe."

Brick's eyes hardened. "Don't say that again. I meant it."

He sounded as though he had meant it. Jeff glanced at his sister. She hadn't said a word, and he knew it must have been hard for her to keep silent. Her hands were tightly locked in her lap, and her face looked strained.

"Let's go on with Doberman's plan," Jeff said slowly. "What's supposed to happen after you and Syl get married?"

"Doberman will continue to run the ranch. Syl will sign over her land to me. I'll sign it over to Doberman, get paid and then ride on."

"What about Wade's share of the range?"

"He'll make some fool play and get killed. His share of the range will then go to Syl, and through me to Doberman."

"So everything goes to Doberman."

"That's the plan, Jeff."

"Syl said that you and Doberman would clash."

He laughed softly. "Sure we will—because I'm going to kick over the traces. I'm not going to have Syl sign over anything to me. She keeps the land. Doberman will never get it through me."

"He'll kill you."

"Not if I can help it—but look at what I'm bucking. First, there's Doberman. I met him when he was riding with King Allenby in the Red River country. He's a wizard with his gun. Then there's Vegas. I've seen him in action three times. I've never seen anyone his equal. There are three more, all top-notch gunslingers—John Creel, Red Murphey and Lou Fiske. Particularly Creel. He's mean as they come. Doberman had another, Traubert, but you took care of him."

"It would be easier to run," Jeff suggested.

Brick leaned back, bracing his hands behind him. He said, "Jeff, I didn't only fall in love with Syl. I fell in love with the Park. I like this high country. I like the trees and the water. I like the idea of living here and raising a family. I grew up on a ranch. I know what it would be like. I could make a go of it, and the past might not hurt me. I did a few things that were wrong, but it was far from here. I doubt if anyone would come this far to get me. At least, I might have a few years. It's worth fighting for."

Jeff hoped, for Syl's sake, that Brick was telling the truth, but to go into the past seemed unnecessary right now. He changed the subject. "How about Wade?"

"I don't know what to do about him," Brick answered. "He's Syl's brother, and yours, but e's still a fool. The only reason he hasn't been illed is that Grandy is still living, and through Vade Doberman can run things. If he had to epend on Syl, she might be a problem."

"How long will Grandy live?"

"Who knows? Doberman could have finished im easily, but he needs him. He needs him ntil Syl and I get married. After Syl and I get narried, Doberman will expect to be able to ontinue his control, through me and the way I andle Syl."

"Then Wade—"

Brick interrupted him. "Let's let Wade go for a ninute. I want to say something about Grandy. Ie looks terrible, I know, but the other night I vent in to see him. He was asleep. A book he ad been reading had fallen to the floor. I picked t up and carried it to the dresser across the oom and left it there. The next morning I emembered the book and went in to get it. I hought he might want it, but he already had it. Vow, how do you suppose he got it? He told me o one else had been in."

Syl caught her breath and straightened up. 'Brick, why didn't you tell me?"

"I shouldn't have told you now. I don't want o give you any false hopes, but I think Jrandy's stronger than most people think.

Maybe he'll never be well, but he's far from dead."

"Then why doesn't he ever talk to me?"

"To understand that, all you have to do is remember the way Grandy treated Jeff."

"You mean—"

Brick was grinning again. He looked from Syl to Jeff, and he said, "Don't you see it? Why you didn't figure it before I can't imagine. Grandy's sick. No question of that, but there is nothing wrong with his head. He knows Doberman is in the saddle. He knows Wade is acting like a fool. He knows, Syl, that you're helpless. When Jeff faced him, he knew that if he didn't disown him he wouldn't live another day. Sure Grandy disowned him, but he did it to save his life."

Jeff was sitting as erect as his sister. What Brick had suggested was something that had never occurred to him. He could see, however, that Brick might have hit on the truth. If Grandy had thought he was in danger, he would have done anything he could to save him. A wave of emotion choked him. Weak, ill and a prisoner in his own home, Grandy still had refused to appeal for help, knowing it would have endangered his son.

"He's quite a man," Brick was saying. "He reminds me of my own father. Crusty, stubborn, honest as they come. He was killed fighting a range hog. He rode in one night with enough lead in his body to have killed several ordinary men, but he lived long enough to warn me and my mother to get away. We did. And I paid his enemies back. That made me an outlaw whether I liked it or not."

Jeff rolled a cigarette using it as an excuse to be silent for a moment. Then he handed the tobacco and papers to Brick.

"Maybe we shouldn't be married Sunday," Syl suggested.

Brick shook his head, sealed his cigarette with the tip of his tongue and said, "No, Syl. We can't stall much longer. We've got to fight—or run."

"What will happen if we get married?"

"Nothing right away, but from then on Wade and Grandy will be in real danger."

"Then I know what to do," Jeff said. It had suddenly come to him. It wouldn't solve the problem or end their trouble, but temporarily it would stop Doberman right where he was.

"Let's have it," Brick said.

"Wade. Wade's the key. Suppose, Brick, that you and Syl get married Sunday and left to take a week's honeymoon, anywhere. And suppose that on Sunday Wade disappears."

Syl looked puzzled. "But why would Wade disappear?"

Jeff grinned. "I'll persuade him. If that happens, he'll be safe from Doberman, and at the same time Doberman won't be able to do anything to

Grandy. Think about it for a minute. You'll see I'm right."

They went on talking for a while, but planning any farther was impossible. Brick complained that Jeff was carrying the heaviest load, but that was questionable, because Brick was constantly under the guns of Doberman's entire crowd.

"Can you get help in picking up Wade?" Brick asked.

"All I need."

"And you'll do it the night of the wedding?"

"That's the time."

"Then just remember—a wedding is a time for celebration. There'll be a lot of drinking. It would be a good time to frame a fight. You killed Traubert. It would be easy for someone to take up his quarrel."

"I'll watch it," Jeff said soberly.

"What if we want to get word to you before the wedding?"

Jeff's answer came instantly and without reservation. "There's a girl in the restaurant you can trust. Gwen Sennett. Leave any message with her."

They left it like that. Jeff walked them to their horses, and before they mounted Syl touched Brick's hand. He looked at her quickly, and the look they exchanged told more of how they felt toward each other than any words would have expressed. It was like an embrace.

"See you in church, at the wedding," Jeff said, smiling. "And good luck to both of you."

He kissed Syl's cheek and shook Brick's hand, then watched them mount their horses and ride away through the trees. A few hours before he wouldn't have believed it possible that Brick and Syl could find any real happiness. But he had been wrong. They owned it now. They were fortunate people.

CHAPTER 14

Jeff left immediately afterward. Keeping under the trees, he slanted toward Latigo Creek. From there, he switched direction, turning north to the Eden River, and he got to the Waldron ranch an hour after dark. Vicki answered his knock. She looked surprised when she saw him, and she stepped back, catching her breath. "I thought it was—that is—"

"You thought it was Wade," he said, guessing.

"Yes. He said he was coming." She took a deep breath, then added, "I wish he wasn't."

Jeff did not try to read anything else into her words. He had steeled himself to whatever might happen. Glancing around the room he asked, "Where are your folks?"

"They went to town, but haven't come back. They said they wouldn't be late. I'm keeping supper warm. Have you eaten?"

"I could take some coffee."

They were just talking, the words unimportant. Jeff could feel the tension between them. He hadn't looked directly at her when he came in, and he wasn't looking at her now, but he knew every line of her face. She was tired, there was hardly any color in her skin and her eyes were shadowed.

He walked to the table and sat down. Vicki poured his coffee, then returned to the stove and stood there silently.

She spoke suddenly, her words low. "I was in town earlier. A man was there. John Creel. They say he was a friend of Bill Traubert's. They say he was waiting for you."

"Forget it, Vicki," he said gruffly.

She whirled toward him. "Why? That's the way things happen. If you kill John Creel, another will take his place. Then another. Then one day you'll be killed."

He looked at her, frowning. "What should I do, Vicki?"

"Go away. Anywhere. You've got to, Jeff."

She was twisting her hands together, leaning forward, breathing hard. He managed a smile and said, "Vicki, it's true I'm facing a certain amount of danger, but Wade is in a worse fix than that. Syl is going to marry Brick Rawson, one of Doberman's riders. She'll sign over her share of the range, which is the same as handing it over to Doberman. Then, if anything happens to Wade, it'll go to Syl and through her to Doberman. Why not worry about Wade?"

A puzzled expression had settled over her face. She shook her head as though she didn't understand—and perhaps she didn't. Perhaps this was too much to pick up, all at once. "Wade hasn't had any trouble with Matt Doberman. I don't know what you mean."

He explained more slowly. "When Grandy dies, half the range will go to Syl, half to Wade. Syl is getting married. She will give her land to her husband, who is one of Doberman's men. If anything happens to Wade, his share of the range will go to her, too. That way, Doberman will have everything."

"But that would be—murder."

"Yes, that would be murder."

"I don't believe it. You're making it up."

"No, I'm not making it up, Vicki. Wade is in serious danger."

She was silent for a moment, then said, "I'll tell him, but what about you?"

"I'll be careful."

She came to the table, her face suddenly coloring. "Jeff, I want you to go away. I want to go with you. I wanted to say it the other night but I was too stubborn, too proud. I'm not proud any longer. I'm just frightened. It's not too late for us. It's always been you and me. Always."

This was what he had been waiting for. This was what he had wanted, but without any strings. He sat rooted where he was, and then he shook his head. "I can't go away, Vicki."

"But why, Jeff?"

"My place is here."

"Even if you get—killed?"

"I don't plan on getting killed."

She came closer and touched him lightly on the shoulder. "Jeff—"

"Don't try to make me change my mind."

Her hand was still on his shoulder. "I was afraid you'd be like this, but there's one thing I can do."

"What?"

"Stand up. I'm not going to argue with you, Jeff."

He got up and stood looking at her. She didn't seem at all angry. She was even smiling. And suddenly he was shaky. He wanted to reach out and grab her, but he didn't. From somewhere, he found the strength to look away.

She spoke again, her voice low, provoking. "What's the matter, Jeff? You used to like me."

That did it. Abruptly she was in his arms and he was kissing her, and it was like old times. But there was a difference now. Half of his mind was still active. Something warned him that it wasn't like Vicki to give up so easily as this. It had even been like that when they had been children. When she wanted something she kept at it. She would seem to give in; then, when they least expected it, she would drive again at what she wanted. And half the time she won.

Something else intruded, the sounds of a horse in the yard. Jeff pushed her away but still held her arms. "That'll be Wade."

She was smiling. "I didn't hear him. Let him go away."

"No. I want to see him."

"But he hates you, Jeff. He's said terrible things about you. He lied about you. When he finds you here—"

"He's probably already seen my horse. Let him in. But, Vicki, don't tell him all I said. Don't warn him about Doberman. It would be like him to challenge him tomorrow."

"You'll stay?"

He grinned. "Wade may not like it."

"I've been nice to him, Jeff, but that was all. And after all, he's your brother. It was just—"

"Keep on being nice to him," Jeff said. And then an experimental question came unbidden to his lips. "Vicki, how much do I owe to my family? Do you think—"

She didn't seem at all surprised. "You owe something to yourself, and to me. I knew you'd see it. We'll talk later."

Wade was at the door, knocking. Vicki turned toward the door, and Jeff watched her, a wry smile crossing his face. What he had just seen wasn't anything unusual. Vicki was running true to the old pattern. She would yield a point, then return to the attack. She meant to have her way. She would always be like that.

At the door Vicki and Wade said something, then Wade brushed past her, acting as though he belonged here. He had adopted a brusque manner that he probably thought fitted a position of authority. His mouth was small and tight-lipped, and he looked angry. "What are you doing here?" he demanded. "Who asked you to stop by?"

Jeff shrugged. "No one."

"The sheriff's looking for you."

"I'll see him some day."

"If you last that long."

Jeff wanted to laugh, but he held it back, because nothing made Wade more angry than a laugh at his expense.

"You're mighty close to the Rocking H line," Wade was saying. "I'd have thought you'd had enough. Paul Lanier's still around."

"He had help," Jeff said. "Toward the end of the fight, someone shoved me off balance."

Wade's face flamed. "You'd say that anyhow."

Vicki stepped between them and spoke, making an uneasy joke. "Hey, you're brothers. I won't have you quarreling."

"He's no brother of mine," Wade snapped.

She took his arm, smiling and leaning toward him. "Please Wade. For my sake, no quarreling."

This should have mollified him, but it didn't. "Tell him to go, Vicki."

"But Wade—"

"That's all right," Jeff said. "I'm going to leave in just a few minutes. How are things going at the ranch, Wade?"

Wade's head came up, and Jeff could sense what

was coming next. Here was a chance to boast, to tell what he had done; it was an opportunity he couldn't miss. "I've done a few things that have been needed for a long time. I moved the Herefords to a higher meadow, where the grass is better. I've cut the herd, too. We weeded out the scrawny stock and sold them. We're making more money than you ever did, or Grandy, either."

"How's your winter feed?" Jeff asked.

"Haven't had the time to do any haying, but there's plenty of time."

"If you don't wait too long, you'll get another full cutting."

Wade showed a flash of irritation. "Don't tell me what to do. I know my job."

Jeff shifted the subject. "How do you get along with Doberman?"

"Just like that," Wade answered, holding up two fingers close together. "Doberman knows what's good for him. I'd fire him in a minute if he crossed me. He knows it, too."

How could you talk to a man like this? Jeff didn't know what to say next. Did Wade actually believe what he had said, or did he secretly know the truth?

"You don't like him, do you?" Wade asked, laughing.

"No, I don't."

"Sure you don't. You think he's crooked, and maybe he is, but I can tell you this. He keeps in line when I'm around. The other men, too."

Vicki was standing at his side, listening. Jeff glanced at her. She was watching his brother, her eyes thoughtful—or perhaps worried.

Wade looked at her, too, then stared at Jeff, his good humor quickly gone. "I thought you said you were going."

"I am," Jeff said. "But don't forget Dutch Meridan."

"Dutch Meridan? He's been dead for years."

Whether Wade would get the point or not, he didn't know. But he decided to try it. "Sure he's been dead for years, but do you remember how he died?"

"Got killed by a bear."

"A pet bear. Dutch caught him as a cub, trained him, made a pet of him. When he got fully grown, folks warned him to be careful, but that didn't worry him a bit. One day, after he hadn't been seen for days, some people went by to find out why. He had been chewed to death."

Wade's face tightened. "Ain't no one gonna chew me up. Don't worry."

"It doesn't hurt to be careful," Jeff said.

He walked to the door. There, Vicki caught him and spoke in a whisper. "Wait until he's gone."

There was a promise in her eyes, in the pressure of her fingers on his arm. He could wait outside for Wade to leave. Vicki would discourage him quickly, send him home. Then he could return, take Vicki in his arms, and it would be old times—with one exception. He would have to change his mind about staying in the Park.

Wade was moving toward them, his eyes dark with suspicion. Jeff looked down at her. He said, "Good night, Vicki. I've a long ride ahead. If I meet your folks on the road, I'll say hello."

She stiffened instantly and drew back. "But I thought—"

He shook his head. "Good-by, Vicki."

Outside he climbed onto his horse and, without looking back, took the road toward town. He felt sick. The chains with which Vicki had held him went far back to his childhood. To break them wasn't easy. But he had done it, and Wade had helped. With Wade there, an argument was impossible—and Vicki had persuasive arguments at her command.

After a few miles he left the road and cut southeast. He would miss the Waldrons that way, but he didn't want to have to talk to them. He didn't want to explain. From here, he would by-pass the town and head for Dan's, and he'd stay there until Sunday, the day Brick and Syl were getting married. Probably until then, nothing much would happen.

CHAPTER 15

Friday the Hotchkiss ranch had a visit from the sheriff. He came alone, stopping at the house to ask where they were, then riding on to the field where they were haying. They had finished their cutting and were racking up when the sheriff arrived, both Jeff and Dan soaking with sweat.

"I could use an extra hand," Dan said, grinning. "Grab a fork and pitch in."

"Can't stay," the sheriff answered. "Glad I can't, too. An hour in the sun would finish me. Just wanted to see Jeff a minute."

"Fire ahead," Jeff said.

"Had an inquest the other day," the sheriff said. "Rightly, you should have been there, but it looked like a clear case of self-defense."

Jeff would have been surprised at any other result. Whatever else he might say about the sheriff, McEllis was straight. He said, "Thanks, Sheriff. I'm not proud of what happened. If it could have been avoided—"

"Something else is worrying me now. Your sister is getting married, Sunday, right after service."

"So I heard."

"Who told you?"

"Things like that get around."

"Then I suppose you know the man she's marrying."

"Brick Rawson."

The sheriff's eyes had narrowed. "I thought you might not like it."

Jeff shrugged. "Maybe I don't, but there isn't much I can do about it. If it's Syl's choice, then I hope she's happy."

"Do you expect to be there?"

"Surely I do. I wouldn't miss it. It wouldn't be right if I did."

The sheriff leaned forward. "You sound like you don't care, and I hope you're right. But let me tell you this, Jeff. If you come to that church and try to cause any trouble, I'll take a hand myself. That's a promise I made to Matt Doberman."

"Does Doberman think I'll cause trouble?"

"Why shouldn't he?"

Jeff was able to smile. "You'll never know I was in the crowd. I won't spoil Syl's marriage."

The sheriff left a few minutes later, and after he rode away they took a little time off to weigh his visit. Jeff put it this way. "His conscience worries him. He's convinced I'm a troublemaker. He's got to prove it."

"Or maybe he's working for Doberman unawares," Dan suggested. "Maybe they want to be sure you're in town."

"At least nothing will happen before the marriage. Doberman wouldn't stand for it."

"And afterwards?"

"Afterwards—anything could happen."

He had told Dan what they were facing. Dan felt they should talk to some others—Nels Gitterhaul and a few more—but they hadn't had the chance. On Sunday they would. Jeff insisted nothing could be done right now. Certainly, however, some of the men in the Park should know the truth and be ready for trouble. This was like a fire that sometimes could be contained and sometimes would spread. No one could guess exactly what was in the future.

They left early Sunday morning. Harriet was excited about the wedding. Although she had been reassured about Brick Rawson, and although she was worried about Jeff, a wedding was still something special. Dan laughed at her and told her to take an extra handkerchief.

"No, I won't cry," Harriet said. "But I'll get— misty. And that's your fault. When a married woman cries at a wedding, it's because she remembers her own wedding day."

"And regrets it?"

"No. She lives it over again. I hope Syl is happy as I am. When will it be your turn, Jeff?"

Jeff laughed. "I'll ask her."

"And who will you ask—Gwen?"

He was startled. How had she guessed? He hadn't thought anyone knew how he felt about Gwen. Certainly, he hadn't talked.

Dan was surprised, too. "Gwen! I didn't even guess."

Harriet seemed pleased. She said, "Dan, use your wits. When Jeff uses her name his voice changes. It softens. And he smiles, and his eyes glow for a minute. I've noticed all the signs. I approve, too. I think she's a fine girl."

"We've got other things to worry about," Jeff said. But he was pleased at what Harriet had said.

They made good time along the road, making it to Crestline shortly after ten.

When they got to the church, they found it was crowded. The circuit preacher usually got a good crowd, but this Sunday the building was jammed. Before eleven every seat, except a few which had been reserved, was taken. The latecomers had to stand around the wall. Nearly everyone from the Park was there, and nearly everyone from town.

In one of the back rows were five men from the Rocking H—Vegas and John Creel, Lou Fiske, Red Murphey and Sol Bealer. Paul Lanier wasn't there, having probably been left home with Grandy. Jeff noticed all five, but he paid special attention to Vegas and Creel.

Vicki was there, too, with her parents. She sat very straight, and she must have known where he was but didn't look toward him. Gwen was across the room, and she smiled when she saw him.

Syl and Brick came in just before the service started. They were followed by Wade and Doberman. A rustle of whispering ran through the room as they appeared, and it was obvious why. Syl looked beautiful, filled with a radiance that glowed in her eyes, in the flush on her cheeks. Brick looked assured, proud, half defiant. He was wearing a new suit and a white shirt, but no gun. Of course, he didn't need a gun. Not yet.

Syl, Brick, Wade and Doberman took the reserved seats in the front, and the service started. It was long, running past the noon hour, but that was understandable. The preacher had a good crowd. He's never had a chance at some of the people here, and he might not get it again.

There was the service, and then the wedding, one running into the other. The wedding was brief. Standing in front of the preacher, flanked by Wade and Doberman, Syl and Brick were married, their answers clear and steady. Then afterwards, half the people there crowded around them, and out in the street someone shouted and started firing his gun. But that was to be expected.

Jeff didn't join the mob. He hung back, watching. If there was any tension in the church, he couldn't feel it. Back at the door were the five

Rocking H riders, but so were many others. Most of the people were smiling, and through the hum of conversation he could hear laughter. Gwen left before he could see her, undoubtedly having hurried away to help her mother at the restaurant. Vicki had also left, with her parents.

He glanced toward Brick and Syl. Although hemmed in by her friends, Syl was motioning him to join her.

He did, and a moment later he shook hands with Brick, then kissed Syl's cheek. She hugged him tightly, then with her lips close to his ear, she whispered, "See Gwen before you leave." No one else heard her words; he was sure of it.

The newly married couple left the church in the traditional manner. They hurried toward the rig at the door, rice showering them as they ran. Shouting men fired their guns in the air. And, as the rig turned down the street, mounted riders swept past it, yelling and blasting their guns. This went on until the rig was outside of town.

"A good send-off," Dan said. "But the celebration is just starting."

He was right. A fight had started near the saloon. The sheriff broke it up, but, as the afternoon wore on and as evening came, there would be other fights. A wedding was an excuse for heavy drinking, and heavy drinking led to trouble.

Henry Newbranch, the grocer, was just past fifty. He was a deliberate man, slow but thorough in his work, slow in his judgments. After dinner he sat in the parlor with Jeff and Dan, and in their talk he indicated that he was uneasy about Matt Doberman. He avoided saying anything about Brick, who now was Syl's husband, but it was evident he was worried.

Mrs. Newbranch called him to the kitchen, and while he was there Jeff turned to Dan. "I've got to go to the restaurant," he explained. "Syl whispered that she had left a message with Gwen."

"Then I'll go see her," Dan said.

"Why not me?"

"No one's after me," Dan replied. "If you go out on the street you might run into John Creel. Use your head, Jeff. If you're careful, you'll have the rest of your life to see Gwen."

Without question, Dan was right. If Creel was looking for Jeff, it would be foolish for him to go to the restaurant.

Nels Gitterhaul came by, and a few minutes later Dan found an excuse to take a walk with him. He was gone half an hour, and when he got back he drew Jeff aside. "I saw Creel on the street," he said. "He was just standing in the shade, watching everyone in sight. Most everyone is getting liquored up, but not him. He's damned sober."

"Wade still in town?"

"In the saloon, playing poker. Nels has got a man keeping track of him. If Wade pulls out of town, we'll hear."

Tonight, in some way or other, Jeff was going to pick Wade up. That was on the calendar. That was why they were still in town.

"What did Gwen have to say?" he asked.

"Syl saw her. She and Brick, Doberman and Wade had coffee before they went to the church. Syl pretended that something was wrong with her dress, and Gwen took her to the kitchen to fix it. There they had a chance to talk. Syl and Brick are going to Grandy's hunting cabin. It's in the hills, west of the ranch. No one now on the ranch knows where it is—except maybe Wade, if he remembers it. And Syl said you knew about it. She told Doberman they'd be gone a week. Then Gwen added something, not a part of the message."

"What?"

"She said that for a week you weren't to bother them. She said if you did she'd break your neck."

Jeff laughed. "I'll bet she would, too. Did she say anything else?"

"Just one other thing. She said she didn't want a dead hero."

It grew dark. The Newbranches were probably surprised their guests hadn't already left, but Dan had found an excuse to wait. He was still looking for help at the ranch, he said, and he had heard of a man who might do. He was waiting to see him. Harriet looked a little worried when Jeff left with him, just after dark, but she asked no questions.

They walked to the river, north and west of town. There Nels joined them. He had brought two horses, and Jeff and Dan were carrying the groceries they had packed and brought in the wagon. These were stowed in the saddlebags.

Nels had the latest report on Wade. He was still in the poker game in the saloon, losing but not losing heavily. He probably planned to stay as long as the game continued. Creel was still in town, and Doberman, too, but Doberman was showing a trace of restlessness. He had sat in a game for a while, but had dropped out.

In planning to pick up his brother, Jeff had had to choose whatever would fit the night. What he had settled on finally was quite simple. He knew Wade's habits. When Wade played poker he liked to drink beer, but he couldn't hold it. Every half-hour or so he would have to go out back, behind the saloon. From one of those trips he wouldn't return.

It had turned colder, and a wind had come up. The smell of rain was in the air, and Jeff hoped it would rain, to wipe out the trail of their horses. Jeff glanced at the others. "Ready?"

Dan nodded, and Nels said, "Let's go pick up that brother of yours."

● ● ●

The yard behind the saloon was partially fenced. On the rear of the lot was an outhouse. Near it was a woodshed, and halfway between the shed and the saloon was a woodpile, which was high and irregular in shape. It was an ideal place for Jeff and the two men with him to hide.

The saloon had a convenient back door. Two men had just used it, and in the next half-hour, half a dozen men went out and in. Then, just as Jeff had expected, Wade had to take a trip outside. But he wasn't alone; Red Murphey was with him, probably because Wade wasn't very steady.

They came directly toward the woodpile, Murphey saying, "Hurry it, Wade. Maybe you'll have better luck in the next hour."

"The cards have been running against me, that's all," Wade said bitterly. "But I'll get even. Just wait and see."

Jeff spoke from the shadows, his voice low but sharp. "Stand where you are. Don't touch your guns. Don't make a sound."

He stood up and moved forward, Dan at his shoulder, Nels just behind. His gun covered the two men.

There was a moment of shocked silence as Murphey stood motionless, his arms half raised, and Wade rocked from side to side. A hoarse cry broke from Wade's throat. "Wh—what do you want? What have I done? I—"

"Turn around," Jeff said harshly.

Wade didn't. He backed away. But Murphey, respecting the guns covering him, turned slowly, careful to keep his hands away from his gun.

Jeff stepped up behind him. His arm jerked up, and then down. The barrel of his gun slammed against the side of Murphey's head, and Murphey spilled to the ground.

Dan lunged past him, hurrying after Wade, who had broken away. He caught him and hauled him down. Nels joined them, and there was a brief struggle. Then they got up, Wade between them, his breath rattling in his throat but no fight left in him.

"We'd better get him away," Dan said. "Who knows when someone will come outside. How about Murphey?"

Jeff glanced at the man on the ground. It was a casual glance, but it saved his life. Murphey had dropped as though he was unconscious, and perhaps he had been out for a few seconds. But he wasn't unconscious now. He was fully awake. He had found his gun—and, cautiously, he was raising it.

There was no time to shout at the others, and no way to avoid what lay ahead. Jeff had reholstered his gun, but he grabbed it again and fired a hurried shot. Murphey's shot screamed past him. Then Jeff heard the man's shrill cry, saw the gun steadying again. He fired once more and Murphey sank back, his gun slipping from his hand.

Murphey was dead. For an instant Jeff stood motionless, staring at the figure on the ground.

Nels grabbed his arm. "Jeff, they'll be here in a minute. Let's get away."

He looked toward the rear of the saloon. No one had shown up yet, but undoubtedly men would soon be crowding into the back yard. He turned and hurried after the others.

Wade had recovered some of his steadiness by the time they got to the river. He had plenty to say, too, most of it in the nature of blustering threats aimed at Dan, Nels and, of course, his brother.

Neither Dan nor Nels had much to say in answer. They boosted Wade into the saddle of one of the horses, then adjusted his stirrups and tied him in place. After this, they stopped for a minute. In leaving, they had heard men out in the yard back of the saloon, but no one had come after them and, probably, no one had seen them. Right now, no one from the saloon could be sure what had happened. A dead man had been found, and Wade was gone. Ironically, it might look as though Wade had killed Murphey and fled.

"What do you think they'll figure, Jeff?" Dan asked.

"I can't even guess," Jeff answered. "We'll

have to see how things work out. If they think Wade killed Murphey, they'll call it a murder. Murphey was a gunslinger. Wade isn't. Besides, Wade's disappeared."

"Then a posse will be after him."

Jeff looked up at the sky. "It's going to rain. We won't leave a trail. Maybe the posse won't find him."

"I can do this, tomorrow," Nels said. "I can get word to the sheriff that one of my men saw Wade streaking toward the pass. That might cool down the search."

"Do it, then," Jeff said. "We can tell the truth later. What we've got to do now is keep Wade where he'll be safe. Dan, tell Gwen what happened."

"I'll tell her," Dan said.

Jeff walked to the other horse. He climbed to the saddle, waved to Dan and Nels and then headed east, leading Wade's horse and ignoring Wade's threats and curses. In about a mile they forded the river, then cut across country. The rain started an hour later, and it came down hard. That was perfect. Their trail to the old Sennett ranch wouldn't be found.

Matt Doberman had missed the excitement behind the saloon. Fifteen minutes before he had left for home, riding alone. He had a job to handle at the ranch.

It had been a good day. Only two things worried him any more. One, of course, was Jeff Carmody. But in a day or two, that worry would be in the past. Bill Traubert hadn't been equal to the job, but John Creel was another matter. Some people figured Creel was as fast as Vegas. When Jeff ran up against Creel, he wouldn't walk away.

The other thing bothering him was Brick Rawson. He had reached some conclusions about Brick. Brick was doing his job and was playing the game, but he had his own angles. Doberman was sure of that. The damned fool had fallen in love with Syl. If he could have done it, he would have taken Doberman's place and made the range his own. Brick Rawson, head of the Rocking H. To hell with that.

It started raining. Doberman got out his slicker, put it on and kept riding. He dismissed his worries. Jeff was going to die; it was only a matter of time. Brick would die, too, but not until he finished his job and handed over the proper papers. Facing a gun, he couldn't do anything else. But Doberman had another plan, too. He could set it up in another week.

He laughed out loud. Brick had been surprised when he hadn't objected to a week's honeymoon. But he had had a reason for letting them go—a damned good reason.

When he got to the ranch he took care of his horse, then went to his cabin. After he had changed his clothes and had a drink he went on to the house. Lanier let him in, his face still swollen from the fight with Jeff.

"How was the wedding?" Lanier asked.

"Just another wedding," Doberman answered. "You can go back to the bunkhouse. I want to see the old man."

He went back there and lit the lamp, then stared at the figure in the bed. Each time he went there he thought he might find Grandy dead. Doberman stepped closer.

"Old man. You still living?" he asked abruptly.

Grandy didn't move, and he didn't look up.

"Old man, I spoke to you," Doberman said. "Are you awake?"

"I'm awake," Grandy said.

Doberman laughed, pleased. They would have another talk. A final talk.

"Just saw the wedding," he said, grinning. "Your daughter Syl and my man Brick. They're married, old man. Off on a honeymoon. When they come back, you know what they'll find. I want to tell you. They'll find you're dead. Too bad."

Grandy looked up, but he didn't speak.

"Yep, you're gonna die tonight, old man. In a couple days we'll have the funeral, then the lawyer in town will open your will and read it. Half the range will go to Wade, half to Syl. I can handle Wade. Brick can handle your daughter. And maybe Wade will have an accident, so all the range will go to Syl. I mean, to Brick. That's the same as saying it's all mine. What you got to say to that, old man?"

"I'll kill you," Grandy said.

"You're not going to have the chance. I don't need you any more. Needed you before to keep Wade or Syl from kicking free. But now Syl's safe, and I'm not worried about Wade. I can snuff him out in a minute."

He raised his head, hearing horses driving into the yard. Some of the men were back from town.

"I'm going to use your pillow, old man," Doberman said. "Never used a pillow before, but I figure it'll work. It'll look, tomorrow, like you just passed out. Good-by, old man. I'll miss you."

He leaned over, then straightened suddenly and turned toward the door. Someone had entered the house and was shouting his name. What the hell had happened? He reached the door and stopped. He saw Creel hurrying down the corridor.

"What's happened?" Doberman asked sharply.

"Murphey's dead," Creel said. "Wade's disappeared. It looked like Wade shot him."

This was incredible. Doberman couldn't believe it. Murphey was damned good with his gun; he wasn't the kind to be caught napping. Wade couldn't even shoot straight.

While he was puzzling over it, Creel went into

detail. They had been in the saloon. Wade had had to go out back, and since he wasn't very steady Murphey had gone with him. Murphey had been cleaning up in the game and had wanted to get Wade back. But out behind the saloon there had been a shot, and, when they got there, Murphey was dead. Wade had vanished.

Matt Doberman was one of the few men in the Park who immediately guessed the truth. Wade hadn't killed Murphey and fled. Instead, it had been Jeff Carmody who had killed Murphey. Wade had been kidnapped. He was sure of it— and he knew something else, too. He had to switch his plans. He had to let Grandy live a few more days. If he killed him now, and if Wade was still away, Syl would be the only active heir to the old man's property. If she and Brick showed up in town, they could kick him off the ranch.

"See you in my cabin in a few minutes," he said bleakly.

Creel left, and after he was gone Doberman walked back to the bed. He stared at Grandy and shrugged, then blew out the lamp and turned away.

He was stopped by a voice from the bed. "Come again, Doberman. Someday I'll be strong enough to get up and kill you."

"Shut up, old man," Doberman said with a snarl. "You haven't got a chance."

CHAPTER 16

Five nights later, and quite late, Jeff rode in at the Hotchkiss ranch and woke Dan from a sound sleep. Harriet got up, too, and stirred up the fire to make fresh coffee. Then she made sure the windows were tightly shaded.

"It doesn't look as though the week has been too hard," Dan said critically.

"But it hasn't been easy," Jeff answered. "Maybe Wade has done some thinking, but I can't see it."

"Did you leave him tied?"

"Nope. It wasn't necessary. I hid his horse and boots. He didn't have a gun."

"And you think that'll keep him?"

"It should. Wade hates snakes. We killed half a dozen right close to the cabin. If I know Wade, he won't step a foot outside."

Dan laughed, then asked, "How about a fire?"

"I took all his matches. For two or three days he'll have to eat out of cans. He's got his knife. What's happened since I left?"

"Just what you thought. The sheriff spent a day hunting for Wade, then got word he had been seen heading for the pass. He's decided now that Wade got away."

"What does Doberman think?"

Dan leaned back. "You know, he surprised me. He figured the truth, then tried to sell it to the sheriff. McEllis wouldn't buy. He can get damned stubborn. Do you know Mike Rawls?"

"He works for Nels, doesn't he?"

"Yep. He's got a scarred face, looks mean, but he's as fine as they come. Nels talked to him, then sicked him on Doberman, and Mike fed Doberman a tale about a hide-out in the high country, north of the Park. Right now, Doberman and several of his men are up there on a wild-goose chase. Nels and another man planted a trail they can find."

Jeff looked from Dan to Harriet. "Where could a man get without friends? I'll never be able to pay up all my debts."

Dan smiled. "You don't owe us a thing. Where are you going now?"

"I'm on my way to see Brick and Syl."

"Is the week over? Don't you remember what Gwen said?"

"I remember," Jeff said smiling. "And I'm getting anxious to see her, but I've got to finish a job first."

"Is it heading that way?"

"Can't see anything else. Doberman's awfully close to what he wants, but he's tottering on the edge of disaster. I'm half afraid of what will happen when they get back. I'm anxious to talk to them."

"When are you riding on?"

"In the morning. When are you going to town?"

"I can go in tomorrow."

"Then I want you to start a rumor. Doberman used a rumor on me, so I'll return it. Set it up with Pops Jelbert, but tell him not to pin it to you. I think you can trust him. Maybe Gwen can spread it. If Nels is in town, his men can help."

"What's the rumor?"

"The truth. I shot Murphey and kidnapped Wade. And in a day or so, we'll ride in. That may forestall any more searching."

"And what will happen in a few more days?"

"Maybe I can tell you after I've seen Brick and Syl," Jeff answered.

He spent the night at the Hotchkiss ranch, then left early in the morning and swung far south. By evening he was in the mountains, but it was Sunday afternoon before he dropped down toward Grandy's cabin. The cabin was in a rugged canyon, choked with shrubbery and watered by a clear, icy stream.

Syl and Brick were still there. He found their horses just below the cabin, and, walking forward, he suddenly saw his sister flying from it, Brick chasing her. He caught her in only a few steps and pulled her down, and then they started wrestling. Jeff, startled at the sight, hurried toward them. Then he heard them laughing, and he stopped, feeling foolish.

Brick saw him and, still holding her down, said, "Hey, Syl. We've got company."

"Send him away," Syl answered. "Tell him we're not home."

"We're not home," Brick shouted.

But he got up, grinning, and pulled Syl to her feet.

Jeff needed only a glance at her face to know how she felt. Her cheeks were pink, and her eyes were sparkling. Her smile had never been wider. If she hadn't been in love before, she surely was now. He couldn't question it. Brick had changed, too, at least temporarily. The twist on his lips didn't have the old ironic edge, and the shell he ordinarily wore had been discarded.

"Maybe I shouldn't have come," Jeff said.

"No, we half expected you," Brick answered. "That was the point in telling you where we were."

Syl's face clouded. "How's Grandy?"

"Nothing new, or Dan would have told me."

"And Wade?"

"Across the Park. Alone, and where he can't get away. He's not happy, but at least he's safe. We had a little trouble the night we picked him up. Murphey's dead."

"One less to worry about," Brick said flatly.

His face had sobered, and he suddenly looked older. The lines around his mouth were there again. Syl, too, looked suddenly weary. They had

had their week, their brief escape. Now the hard realities of life had to be faced.

They had the rest of the afternoon, though, and the evening. Brick and Syl showed Jeff the two trophies they were bringing home. Brick had killed a bear and had saved the skin for curing, and Syl had brought down an eleven-point deer. They had preserved the antlers.

They had had a wonderful time. "And two or three times a year, we're coming here for a week," Syl said positively. "It's a pledge we've made to each other."

It was a pledge they might not be able to keep. Matt Doberman, and a few others, stood in the way.

It was evening. They had discussed what to expect from Doberman, but this wasn't getting them anywhere. Jeff paced the cabin restlessly, while Brick and Syl sat at the table. Syl looked tired. Brick reached for her hand, squeezed it and then said, "Jeff, you've got a plan. I can feel it."

"Yes, I've got a plan," Jeff admitted. "It might work, or it might not. A lot depends on Syl."

She looked up quickly. "I'll do whatever you say. We talked about it, Brick and I. He's not going to be foolish about me. I'm caught in this, the same as the rest of us."

Jeff took another turn around the room.

"When are you two going home?" he asked abruptly.

"We'll leave tomorrow morning," Brick answered. "We can get home by dusk."

"I don't like you going home," Jeff said. "But to do anything else would bust things wide open. Grandy wouldn't have a chance. We'd have to ride on the Rocking H, and a good many people might get hurt. Do you think you can go home safely?"

Brick was thoughtful. "Doberman's suspicious of me, I know. But he needs me for a while. I think we can risk it."

"Then you will get home Monday evening. Take it easy Tuesday. You'll hear I kidnapped Wade, maybe that I killed him. How they'll tell the story I don't know—but Syl, when you hear about it, I want you to be bitter. I want you to say you hate me."

Syl nodded. "Yes, I can say that."

"You'll hear this, too. You'll hear that I'm giving myself up to the sheriff, that I'll ride in Wednesday noon. Brick, what do you reckon will follow?"

Brick poured fresh coffee. "I'd reckon Doberman will be there, and with most of his men. But what will happen to you? If the sheriff gets his hands on you, he'll slap you in jail."

"No, I don't think he will. But that's not the important thing. I want Syl to be present. Who owns the Rocking H?"

"Grandy."

"Sure, Grandy. He's been sick. Wade's been

acting for him. But, since Wade is gone, who can speak for Grandy?"

Syl came quickly to her feet. "I could, Jeff."

"That's it exactly, Syl. There will be a crowd at the sheriff's office, many of them my friends. I want you to live up to your father. In front of everyone there, I want you to fire Matt Doberman and everyone riding for him. Tell them to get out. You have the authority to do it. Wade won't be there to question it, and Grandy won't be there. You are the owner's daughter. Doberman's nothing but a foreman. Everyone there will have to back you up."

"And how will Doberman take it?" Brick asked quietly.

Jeff shook his head. "I don't know. He can't challenge Syl's right to fire him. He can appeal to Wade, but Wade won't be there. He can't appeal to Grandy. He's too sick."

"He can fight."

"Then he'll be bucking the law. He'll be finished."

"No, it won't be as easy as that," Brick insisted. "And I'm not sure how it'll work out. But I'm willing to try it. I'll be right there to help. It'll do one thing, at least—it'll bust everything wide open."

They talked a while longer, then Jeff insisted he had to leave. Brick walked outside with him to is horse. He was worried about the part Syl had to carry. "I wish we could have left her out of t," he said heavily. "If Doberman sees he's whipped, he may hit out in every direction."

"Worry about yourself," Jeff answered. "I'll see hat Syl's protected—but what about you? No natter what else happens, Doberman and his entire crowd will be after you. They'll look on you as a traitor. You were one of them, and turned against them."

"That had to happen," Brick said indifferently. Then he laughed softly. "We finally got on the same side, didn't we?"

"Looks that way."

"Syl made the difference. I've been a lucky man. We've had a week I could never tell you about. We tried to pack a lifetime into it."

There was a fatalistic note in his voice that Jeff didn't like. "Don't be a damned fool, Brick," he said gruffly. "Syl's going to live a long time. What about the years ahead? I want to find out if you can run a ranch."

This struck Brick funny, and his laugh rang out. "Maybe I'll show you. I actually know a little about ranching. We'll see what happens."

Jeff rode through the night, and by the next evening he had made it to the Hotchkiss ranch. He was worn out from the trip. On the way he had figured out a dozen things that could wreck his plan, none of which made him feel any easier.

"We're ready, Dan," he said soberly. "We want to put on a show in Crestline, Wednesday noon, at the sheriff's." He explained his plan, and then added, "I'll need help. I want a crowd in town. I want a dozen men who can be loaned to Syl after she's fired Doberman. I want them in town at the sheriff's office to back her up when she takes a hand. And I want men like Abe Waldron, Risling, Newbranch, Zeigler and a few of the leaders to be present."

"Don't worry about that," Dan answered. "Should I tell the sheriff you'll be there, Wednesday noon?"

"Yes. Make it definite, and spread the news. I'll get to town tomorrow night. I'll have to find a place."

Dan grinned. "How about Gwen's?"

He looked up, startled.

"Don't worry—Gwen's mother will be there," Dan said, laughing. "But I'm sure it would be all right. Gwen told me the other day you were to use her home any time you wished. She said if no one was there the key was under the third flower pot on the right side on the porch. Now, what are you going to do until you head for town?"

"I want to be sure Wade's still safe."

"That means another long ride."

"Can't help it."

He borrowed some extra food, then rode on, making it to the old Sennett ranch the next morning. Wade hadn't moved from the house. He hadn't shaved, and he was dirty. He begged to get away, promising to leave the Park. He would have promised anything.

Facing him again hadn't been pleasant, and Jeff didn't stay long. "You've got to remain here two more days," he told him. "After that, I'll send for you. And you don't have to leave the Park. You're going to be needed home."

"All I did was take Grandy's place," he answered, showing a flash of anger. "What was wrong with that?"

"I suppose you put Grandy's shoes on too soon," Jeff answered. "You started too young."

"I'm as big as you are."

"Size doesn't have a thing to do with it." Then Jeff stared at Wade. "Wade, do you believe a thing I've told you about Doberman?"

"I don't think he's as bad as you say. I was going to fire him anyhow."

"And how would you fire a man like Doberman?"

Wade bit his lips. "I suppose you think I'm afraid of him. Well, I'm not. I'd have fired him. You didn't give me a chance."

What would happen to Wade? Jeff didn't know. He wasn't temperamentally suited to run a ranch, and he couldn't handle authority. He couldn't think straight, and he didn't have the patience to plan. He didn't like to work, either, or stir up a sweat. He didn't like to get dirty. He hadn't changed a bit from the time he was thirteen or fourteen, when he had wanted to do nothing but take it easy. Wade might grow up, but Jeff could see no signs of it.

CHAPTER 17

In the hills, and away from the ranch, Jeff got several hours rest, and then he started for town. It was late when he got there, but he still avoided the main street, anxious not to be seen. There was a stable behind the Sennett home. He left his horse there, then went to the door.

Mrs. Sennett admitted him. She said, "Come in, Jeff, I've been expecting you. Dan said you were coming. You're to stay here until Dan joins you in the morning."

Jeff thanked her, then looked around the room. Gwen wasn't in sight, nor could he hear her. He asked where she was.

"Carrie Ibberton hasn't been well," Mrs. Sennett explained. "Gwen offered to stay with her until her husband gets home. That will be after midnight. She'll see you in the morning. I'll show you your room."

He was disappointed, but it couldn't be helped. "Thanks, Mrs. Sennett," he said, following her.

She was giving him Gwen's room. He guessed that immediately, and after she left he examined it critically. The room was spotlessly clean, no dust anywhere.

He got to bed, blew out the lamp and then lay awake, listening for Gwen's footsteps. The bed had been changed, but in spite of that it came to him gradually that he could catch the faint scent of her presence, and his imagination was stirred. He decided abruptly he wouldn't be able to sleep a wink, but he was wrong. Long before Gwen got home he was asleep.

She knocked on the door early in the morning, and came in with a cup of coffee.

"I listened at the door," she said, smiling. "Heard you stirring. There's no reason you have to get up, but some men aren't fit to live with in the morning until they've had their coffee."

"I can be nasty either way," Jeff said, grinning.

She set the coffee on the stand, then stood looking down at him, her hands on her hips. She probably had had very little sleep, but she didn't seem tired.

"Come closer," Jeff said.

"Not yet. How did you sleep?"

"There's a bump in the bed."

"I don't think it bothered you. When I looked in, you were sleeping like a baby."

Jeff sat up, bracing his hands behind him. "You were in last night! When?"

"It was quite late," Gwen said, laughing. "And mother thought it was terrible. You weren't snoring. I liked that."

Jeff sat straighter. "Come here, Gwen."

Still laughing, she shook her head. "No. Not yet."

226

"But why?"

Her face changed, turning quite serious. "You have a job this morning. I don't know exactly what it is, but I'm quite sure it's dangerous. I don't think anything else should interfere."

"But this wouldn't interfere."

"Yes it would, Jeff. I'm not just an incident. If you're thinking about me I don't want you to be thinking about anything else. It's got to be like that."

Damned if she wasn't right. He managed a smile. "I've got to see the sheriff, about noon. Doberman will be there, and Syl and Brick. And a few others. We hope to settle things. Then what should I do?"

"Then it'll be up to you. I'm not going any place."

"I'll be in to see you."

She turned quickly around, but at the door she stopped, looked back and then spoke in a rush. "Jeff, I'd like to say many things, but I mustn't. All morning I'll drop dishes all over the restaurant. I'll be that nervous. Don't keep me waiting too long."

He didn't see her again during the morning. By the time he was dressed she and her mother had left for the restaurant. They had left the house to him.

The morning passed slowly, and Jeff spent it

pacing the house restlessly. He couldn't know exactly what would happen when they faced the sheriff. A great deal depended on Syl—on her firmness and the words she would use. A great deal depended on Brick. And on how Doberman reacted. Either in the sheriff's office, or outside in the street, or somewhere in town, there would be a flurry of violence. It was inevitable. What was going to happen today would smash Doberman's plans, but he wasn't the kind to take it lying down. There wasn't any question of that.

Dan got to the house just before noon. Nels was with him, and both looked satisfied.

"Everything's ready," Dan said. "We've got more than a dozen men spotted along the street. They know what's up. No one will start anything, but if there's any shooting they're ready. Newbranch will be at the sheriff's office in a minute or two, and Abe Waldron and Zeigler will be with him. The sheriff's waiting, but I've heard he doesn't think you'll show."

"How about Doberman?"

"He rode in about half an hour ago. Vegas was with him, and Creel, Fiske and Bealer."

"Brick and Syl?"

"Haven't seen them yet. I suppose they'll ride in together. They may be here now."

"Check on it, Dan," Jeff said, frowning. "It's damned important to be sure they're here."

Dan agreed. "I'll take a look." Then he left the house.

The noon hour came and passed. Standing at the window, Jeff watched anxiously. It was ten after twelve when he saw Dan hurrying to join them, and his news wasn't good. As far as he could tell, Brick and Syl hadn't yet reached town.

"We'll just have to wait," he said bleakly. "Damn it, Jeff, where are they? They know what time it is."

"Yes, we'll have to wait," Jeff agreed. "But we can't wait forever."

Again he paced the floor, and the strain of waiting wasn't easy. It got to be twelve-twenty, then twelve-thirty. A man stationed on the street was supposed to let them know the minute Brick and Syl came in sight. But the man didn't come, and at twelve-thirty-five Jeff snapped his watch shut and turned to the door.

"Dan, we can't wait any longer," he said slowly. "Brick and Syl might still get here, but I'm no longer counting on them."

"They ran out on us," Dan said bitterly.

Jeff shook his head. He was sure that wasn't it. Brick wasn't the kind to run, and neither was Syl. Nor were they late. The explanation was something else, and he thought he knew what it was. Doberman was smarter than he had thought; he had smelled a trap. Without much doubt, Brick and Syl were prisoners back home.

"What are we going to do at the sheriff's?" Nels asked.

"As much as we can," Jeff answered. "I don't know what will happen now, but I've got to go ahead. Doberman will be there. I can say a few things."

"We'll back you, Jeff," Dan said quietly.

"Go as far as you want," Nels growled.

Their encouragement helped. They left the house and walked to the main street. The sun, straight overhead, burned down on Jeff's shoulders, and there wasn't even a slight breeze to make the heat more bearable. But he hardly noticed it. Even without Brick and Syl, he could do half the job at least.

At the corner they turned toward the sheriff's office. A crowd was waiting there, out in front. He picked out Doberman, flanked by Vegas and Creel. Newbranch was there, and Abe Waldron and Zeigler. Risling was there, too, and Hap Ibberton from the saloon.

Vicki appeared suddenly on the street. She came out of the store just ahead, and Jeff knew it wasn't by accident. He could sense that she had been waiting and watching for him. She was pale and tense, but determined. As they got nearer she raised her arm and called, "Jeff, I've got to see you. Right now."

It sounded like a command, although she probably hadn't meant it that way. Jeff touched his hat and smiled. "Sorry, Vicki. I can't stop now. Later—"

"You'll have no chance later."

"Then I won't, Vicki."

They walked on past her, and now Jeff was frowning. He was afraid he hadn't been very courteous, but he hadn't been able to help it. Vicki should have known he wouldn't stop.

"Notice how Doberman's got his men stationed?" Nels said under his breath. "Two men close to him, two on the fringe. Hit the ground if anything happens."

Jeff had noticed the setup himself, but he managed a shrug. Plans didn't always work out.

It was the sheriff who started the talking. As they got to the crowd he stepped forward. His words came sharply. "Jeff, you're under arrest. I'll take your gun."

"But not right away," Jeff answered. "Before I hand over my gun, I want to know why I'm being arrested."

"Two charges," the sheriff said shortly. "Kidnapping and murder. Or maybe it's double murder. Maybe Wade's dead."

"He wasn't dead yesterday."

"Prove it."

Jeff waved his arm easily. "I don't have to. Who said Wade was kidnapped? Maybe he took a trip."

Doberman could keep silent no longer. He thrust forward to stand with the sheriff, and he sounded angry. "We're just wasting time. Everyone knows Wade was kidnapped."

Jeff looked straight at him. "Suppose you prove it. Did you see it happen? How do you know I kidnapped my brother? I want facts."

Doberman was momentarily stumped. Glancing to the side, he caught sight of Lou Fiske. He pointed at him. "Fiske, you heard that Wade was kidnapped. Who told you?"

"Heard it in the saloon from Hap Ibberton," Fiske said.

Doberman looked at Ibberton. "Where did you get it?"

"From Pops Jelbert," Ibberton said.

"Where did you get it, Jelbert?"

The barber grinned. "Heard it from Fiske when he came in for a shave."

They were back where they had started. Several men in the crowd were laughing, but Doberman's face was ugly. "I still say we're wasting time. I know Wade was kidnapped. What else could have happened to him?"

"I'll tell you what happened," Jeff said.

He paused and looked down the street. Brick and Syl weren't in sight. And they weren't coming. He could be sure of that now.

"Jeff, we're listening," the sheriff was saying. "Where's your brother?"

"Well, it's like this," Jeff said slowly, being very careful of his words. Temporarily, it wouldn't put Brick and Syl in a very good light, but that couldn't be helped. "Wade came to see me Sunday. He was worried. Syl had just married Brick Rawson, and Brick was one of Matt Doberman's crowd. He—"

"That's got nothing to do with it," Doberman shouted. "You're just—"

"Will you shut up a minute?" Jeff said sharply.

"No, by God. I won't!"

Doberman's hand had dropped closer to his gun. He knew what Jeff was going to say and he wanted to stop it, even at the risk of a fight.

But the sheriff broke it up. He swung between the two men, and his voice held a note of authority. "Hold back, Doberman. Jeff's not going any place. I want to hear what he's got to say."

Jeff glanced at the others. Newbranch was leaning forward, listening, his eyes wide with interest. Everyone else was watching him, too. Jeff knew what he was going to say. He knew he couldn't prove it, but what he said would be remembered—and that was half the victory.

"You can see it easily," he said slowly. "When Grandy dies, half his range will go to Syl, half to Wade. Syl is married to one of Doberman's men. Through him, Doberman can control her half of the range. Then, if Wade has an accident and gets killed, his land will go to her. That will give Doberman the entire shebang. Wade was afraid he'd get killed. That's why he disappeared."

Before he finished talking, Doberman was shouting that it wasn't true. He reached out and swept the sheriff aside, his hand dropping to his gun. He would have drawn it, but before he could two men closed in and grabbed his arms. The same thing was happening to Vegas and John Creel, and on the fringes of the crowd Bealer and Fiske stood rigid, each feeling a gun at his back. The men chosen by Dan and Nels had done an effective job.

It took the sheriff only another moment to assert his position. "There's gonna be no shooting," he ordered crisply. "I'll drop the first man to reach for his holster."

"It's all a pack of lies," Doberman shouted.

"Then we'll prove it," the sheriff answered.

"How?"

"Find Wade. See what he's got to say." He whirled to face Jeff. "Where's your brother?"

"I'll have him here in two days," Jeff said. "But you've got to give him protection."

He stared at Doberman, deliberately grinning. The men who had been holding Doberman had released his arms, but they could grab him again, and he must have known it. And then he realized that Jeff had friends here in Crestline. How many he couldn't be sure, but maybe too many.

Staring straight at the sheriff, Doberman repeated his denial of Jeff's charge. "Everyone here knows I got along all right with Wade," he insisted. "When he gets here, you'll hear it from his own lips—if you ever see him. I figure Wade is dead. I figure Jeff is trying to horn in on the Rocking H. As far as Brick Rawson is concerned, I never saw him before he came to the Park. He's not my man. He never was."

He broke away, angling across the street toward the saloon. Vegas and Creel followed him, and behind them came Fiske and Bealer. Fiske was kicking up dust. He looked back, obviously uneasy.

"Jeff," the sheriff said stubbornly. "Where's Wade?"

"I can't tell you," Jeff answered. "But I'll have him here in two days."

"Is that a promise?"

"Yes."

"Don't see why you can't tell me. And anyhow, that was a crazy thing you said to Doberman. If it's true, he ought to be in jail."

"That's where he ought to be," Jeff said.

He spoke to Abe Waldron, Risling, Newbranch and several of the others who were still around. In these men, with those Dan and Nels had organized, he had a crowd three times as large as Doberman's. Right now, with the co-operation of the sheriff, they could close in on the saloon, disarm the men inside and put them under lock and key.

And why not? He toyed with the idea; then, glancing down the street, he caught his breath. A rider had come in sight at the far end of the street and had reined up for a moment, as though unsure of what to do. Jeff strained his eyes, not wanting to believe what he was seeing. The man at the end of the street was his brother—sagging in the saddle, unshaven, unclean. He hadn't been recognized yet, but it wouldn't be long before he was.

Jeff quickly weighed the possibilities. In another minute, word would be passed around that Wade was here. Immediately then, the sheriff would question him, and he knew what Wade would say. There wasn't any possibility that Wade would back him up, because here was his chance to get even. Before Wade got through talking, Jeff would be in jail.

That was something Jeff couldn't afford. He was sure that Brick and Syl were in serious danger. There was a possibility that they were dead, but he didn't think Doberman would have gone that far. More likely they were prisoners, and if he could get to them he might be able to get them away. That had been his next plan, after deciding what to do about Doberman. Now it necessarily came first.

He drew Nels and Dan to one side, and spoke hurriedly. "Keep your men together and out of trouble. Who owns that bay across the street?"

"It belongs to one of Zeigler's men, I think," Nels said.

"I'm borrowing it," Jeff said. "Explain it to him."

"But where are you going?" Dan asked.

"I'll tell you now," Jeff answered. Then he raised his voice. "Hey, sheriff. I'm going after Wade right now."

"Don't waste any time," answered the sheriff.

Jeff swung away, running as he cut across toward the bay. Down at the other end of the street, two men were at Wade's side, and one was waving and shouting. Jeff pulled the reins free, hauled himself into the saddle and streaked in the other direction. He knew he was leaving Nels and Dan in a bad fix, but at least they weren't in physical danger. Doberman might talk a lot after Wade had told his story, and he might make a lot of noise. But, if he expected to earn a respectable place in the Park, he wouldn't resort to unnecessary violence.

Heading south, Jeff looked back again. A crowd was gathering around his brother.

CHAPTER 18

For several miles, Jeff held to the road, but when he was well out of sight he aimed straight toward the Rocking H. Anyone following him would surely pick up his trail, but he didn't have time to worry about that. The only important thing now was to get to the ranch before Doberman did. And he might head that way. He might easily guess where Jeff was going.

Throughout the entire ride, Jeff worried that Doberman might beat him home, but there was no sign of him when Jeff came in view of the buildings. The place seemed deserted, and the yard was empty of saddled horses. He rode on, slanting toward the trees screening Bear Trap Creek to a point behind the barn.

He left his horse there and checked his gun, then reviewed what he had been planning. So far as he knew, and without counting Brick or Wade, Doberman had only five men. Four had been with him in town. That left one other—Paul Lanier. At a guess, then, Lanier was here at the ranch. What Jeff had to do was get him, and he couldn't waste any time doing it. At any minute, Doberman might ride in, with or without the sheriff.

Jeff walked up behind the barn, circled to one

of the front corners, then streaked toward the house. Lanier had been inside when he had come here before. He was probably there now, and, if he had been looking through the window, he could have cut Jeff down. But nothing like that had happened. Jeff circled to the back door and saw that the latch was fastened. He moved on, swinging around the west wing. There were several open windows, all screened, but Syl's was still torn from his previous visit. He loosened it and climbed inside. A figure was on the bed— his sister. She was on her side, her back to him, her wrists and ankles bound.

He crossed to the door and closed it, then turned to the bed. Stooping over, he spoke in a whisper. "Quiet, Syl. I'll have you free in a minute. Don't make a sound."

She looked around, and her face was tragic, tear-streaked. Her eyes were wide in a vacant stare. Or perhaps it was shock that had gripped her—or fear.

He drew a knife from his pocket and cut the rope around her wrists, then moved to her ankles.

She spoke suddenly. "They killed him."

"Brick?"

Her voice was shaky. "They took him away— then I heard a shot. They came back and said he had double-crossed them. They laughed about it."

This didn't sound right. If they had killed Brick Rawson, how did they expect to control her or gain title to her land? It was unrealistic to think she would marry anyone else. They had needed Brick. He was the key to the entire plan.

"Stay right where you were," he said slowly. "I'll take care of Lanier. Then we'll get away."

He stepped to the door and listened; then he opened it and moved into the hall. They had kept their voices low, and he didn't think Lanier could have heard them. He glanced back at Grandy's room. The door was open. If they had the time, he wanted to see Grandy, but he couldn't think of it now. Lanier came first. He drew his gun, then edged toward the front room.

He was just beyond the door to his old room when he heard someone behind him. He thought it was Syl, trailing him, and he looked around. He was wrong. It was Paul Lanier. The man must have heard him and stepped into Jeff's old room. Now, as Jeff turned, Lanier was on him, a gun barrel slamming at his head. He tried to duck, and he tried desperately to whip his gun around. But he was unsuccessful. The gun barrel crashed against his skull. He felt a blinding pain, and then for a time he knew nothing.

When he awoke he was in the barn, lying face down on the ground, his legs and arms bound so tightly he couldn't move them. It was still light, an indication that he hadn't been unconscious very long, if that was important. But it wasn't. There wasn't a chance he could get away.

His head throbbed from the blow on his skull, and his stomach churned, making him feel sick. He was disgusted at the way he had been tricked. Perhaps it had been a natural thing to figure it had been Syl behind him in the hall, but in a situation like that a man couldn't afford a single mistake. Now he would stay where he was until Doberman got home. After that—

It wasn't pleasant to wonder what Doberman would do. He twisted, turning on his side, then raised his head. He wasn't alone in the barn. Brick was here. And he wasn't dead. Syl had been wrong about that. Brick was standing against one of the struts below the hayloft, tied there, his arms behind his back.

Jeff called, "Brick—"

"Wondered how long you'd sleep," Brick answered. "How did Lanier get you?"

"I rode in to get you and Syl. Didn't make it."

"We didn't make it to town, either. Doberman figured something was wrong. I should have been ready for him."

"He told Syl you were dead."

"Sure. He's trying to break her down. Tonight he'll resurrect me, figuring that by then Syl will be ready to sign anything to save our lives."

"How would that work?"

"The papers will be dated ahead. Then they'll kill us, but they'll say we went on a trip. Later on, a letter will be sent through the mails to Doberman. It'll be from some distant town, saying we're not returning and that we want to sell our property in the Park. After that, the papers will be produced."

"What will you do?"

"What can I? Maybe I can put up a fight, but it won't amount to much. I've been tied here so long, and so tight, I haven't got any feeling in my hands. If someone cut me free and gave me a un, I couldn't hold it." He sounded hopeless He looked older, tired.

"Maybe I can do something," Jeff said vaguely. "How was Syl?"

"Like you would expect. She's quit fighting."

"She hadn't been hurt?"

"No."

"At least I can be thankful of that. I wish—" Brick broke off. He raised his head, listened and then added, "Here they come. Time's running out."

Jeff had heard the same sounds, the drumming of hoofbeats. How many were coming he couldn't tell—but not many, probably not a posse. The horses pulled into the yard, and he caught the murmur of voices. Then a moment later Doberman came in, followed by Vegas,

Creel, Bealer, Fiske and. Lanier. Wade was there, too, but no one else.

Lanier was wearing his wide grin. "I saved him for you, Matt. Could have finished him. What's it worth to me?"

"We'll see about that later," Doberman said.

He walked forward, a satisfied glint in his eyes. Back in town, and after the session in front of the sheriff's office, he had been a shaken man, desperate, putting up a front. But he had changed since then, since Wade had appeared. He was riding high once more.

"So you walked right in, Jeff," he said, grinning. "Nice of you. Saves trouble."

"I'll save you no trouble," Jeff answered.

"But you will. Grandy's been hanging on too long. You came out here, went to his room and started a ruckus. That's where the sheriff will find your body, sprawled over the dead body of the old man."

Wade stiffened, looking surprised. "Hey, Doberman. What do you mean? I don't think—"

"Who asked you to think?" Doberman said bitingly. "Go take a ride—see your girl. And don't get in my way."

Wade stood on the brink of a high precipice, and he knew it. Jeff could see it in his face. Wade could deceive himself no longer. Now he knew what Doberman was planning in the next few minutes. He could see the full extent of his purpose there at the ranch. He knew if he turned away he was lost, and if he stayed he was lost. He was now looking at the truth, and its face was ugly. Perspiration glistened on his forehead, stood around his mouth. His lips moved, but he didn't seem able to speak.

"Do what I said," Doberman said heavily. "Take a ride. I'll look after things."

A mumbling voice finally came from Wade's throat. "I can't go any place like this. These borrowed boots are too tight. I gotta change clothes."

Doberman laughed. He would have no more trouble with Wade. Whenever he spoke, Wade would jump. He said, "All right, go change your clothes, but hurry. Creel, cut those ropes around Jeff's ankles. We'll take him to the house. Brick, too. Maybe Syl's ready to bargain."

Creel cut the bonds around Jeff's ankles, then pulled him erect, his wrists still tied. Fiske was freeing Brick from the strut. The others drifted to the door, but waited there. Wade slipped past them and disappeared in the direction of the house.

"Not a pleasant end," Brick said bitterly.

He could scarcely stand, so Fiske steadied him and said in a growling voice, "Don't try anything with me, Brick. I'll use my gun if I have to."

They moved to the door and joined the others, then stepped outside and started for the house.

They were halfway there when Wade, ahead of them and at the steps, suddenly stopped. He was staring at the door.

Jeff stopped where he was, and so did everyone with him. They stared at the porch and at the figure that had appeared there. It was Grandy—thin and gaunt and probably terribly weak, too. But he had a gun in each hand, and he was covering the men in the yard with them. Then he spoke, and there was nothing weak about his voice. It came out in an angry roar. "What's going on? Who tied up Jeff—my son?"

No words, anywhere, could have sounded any better to Jeff. He straightened, feeling a sharp lift. There was nothing wrong between him and Grandy. What had been said in his room could be forgotten. Grandy had never meant it. Brick had been right—Grandy had disowned him to save his life.

"Another thing I want to know," Grandy shouted. "I found my daughter tied in her room. Who did it?"

Syl had come outside to join him. She had a gun, too, but when she saw Brick her face lit up with wonder. She started toward him, but Grandy said something to her. She stopped and stood watching the others in the yard.

Jeff glanced at the men around him. Everyone was tense. Several of the men had their hands on their guns, but no one had risked a shot.

Everyone was waiting for someone else to make the first break.

Doberman spoke under his breath. "Watch him close. He's an old man, too weak to stand up long."

Weak Grandy might be, but he didn't show it. He raked a glance at Wade, then barked, "Wade! Why are you just standing? Cut your brother free. Brick, too. Get a move on."

"Right away," Wade answered, and he seemed glad at the order. Turning, he hurried toward them, circling behind Jeff. He took out his knife and started sawing on the rope around Jeff's wrists.

Grandy spoke again, the words harsh. "Doberman. Come closer."

The man sucked in his breath. He took a step forward, then stopped.

"Come closer," Grandy thundered. "Do you want me to shoot you where you are?"

Doberman took another step, then started talking. It was obvious he was stalling, waiting for Grandy to weaken. He called, "Grandy, you got things all mixed up. If you'll only listen a minute—"

"I've listened plenty," Grandy answered. "You've come to my room many times. You called me old man. I don't like being called old man. But I made you a promise. Remember?"

Doberman was several steps in front of the rest

of them now, standing motionless, his right hand still on his gun. In a moment he was going to whip it up. Jeff could sense it. He pulled on the bonds around his wrists. Wade was sawing on the rope, but he was either deliberately slow or had a terribly dull knife.

"Don't anyone else interfere," Grandy shouted. "Doberman, this is for you. This is what I promised."

Doberman jerked up his gun but he didn't have a chance. A bullet shattered his right arm. Grandy fired again, this time hitting his left arm. Doberman started screaming. Two more shots followed, aimed at Doberman's legs. He pitched to the ground, still screaming, his body twitching and rolling from side to side.

"How do you like it now?" Grandy roared from the porch. "Call me old man, huh? Take my ranch, huh? Never, Doberman. Not you, or all your men."

He fired again. Doberman's screams ended abruptly. His body settled down, and he didn't move again.

Jeff's hands were finally free, but he still held them behind his back, noticing exactly where everyone else was standing. They weren't out of this yet. Doberman was finished, but Vegas, Creel and the others were still armed and dangerous. It might be that under the guns of Grandy and Syl they would surrender. But they might not. They could guess what they would face if they did. They had had a part in holding Grandy prisoner. What would happen to them was obvious. The men here in the Park had a stern code of justice.

Vegas and Creel were off to Jeff's left, but Brick was between them and him. Bealer, Fiske and Lanier were on his right. Wade, still behind him, had forgotten about freeing Brick. He was staring, fascinated, at Doberman's body. Jeff edged slightly to the right. Bealer, with a left-hand draw, was wearing his gun where Jeff might be able to get it. But to get it and whirl on Vegas and Creel wouldn't give him a chance if they moved at the same instant. And what of the three other men?

Jeff glanced at Brick, who caught his eye and nodded. And then he said, "Any time, Jeff."

What he meant by that Jeff didn't know. He looked toward the house. Grandy had backed to the wall, and was leaning there. His gun still looked steady, but he was undoubtedly feeling the strain of his weeks in bed. He was saying something to Syl, and now Syl spoke, her voice high and shrill. "Throw down your guns. Right now."

For an instant, no one moved. Then Creel spoke, his voice low. "Take him, Vegas. I'll handle—"

He didn't get to finish. Brick swung toward him, driving straight at him. Jeff grabbed Bealer's gun, and as he swung around he heard the sharp explosion of Creel's gun. Creel had turned, but Brick had hit him as he fired, jarring his aim. His shot sailed past Jeff's shoulder, and behind him someone yelled.

Beyond Brick and Creel, who now were on the ground, Vegas twisted toward Jeff. Jeff fired, then fired again. His bullets drove the man backward. Vegas turned around, dropping to the ground. Bealer's arms were in the air, and he was screaming that he had given up, but Fiske hadn't. He was firing at the two on the porch. Jeff dropped him, then saw Lanier folding over and holding his stomach. Turning on his knees he saw that Creel had rolled free and was raising his gun. He had two shots left, and he let Creel have them. Then he scrambled toward the man to get his weapon.

But he didn't need it. Suddenly the fight was over. For Doberman it had been over some time before, but now Vegas, Creel, Fiske and Lanier were on the ground. Only Bealer had surrendered, and not far away Wade was covering him with a gun. What part Wade had had in the battle Jeff didn't know, but at least he was helping now. Jeff looked toward the porch. Grandy was still on his feet, no longer leaning against the wall, and Syl was running toward Brick.

"Seems like you did all right," Brick said, sitting up.

Jeff made no answer. He didn't feel like it. He still was alive, thanks to the reckless way Brick had acted and to Grandy's shooting, and Syl's, and the way things had worked out. It could have had a different ending just as easily.

Syl dropped down at Brick's side, and Jeff heard her anxious questions; then he heard Grandy shouting again from the porch. "Jeff, get on your feet! Clean up this mess in the yard."

Jeff had to grin, even though he didn't feel like it. "Right away, Grandy," he replied, and he stood up. "Go back inside. Take it easy."

"I've been taking it too easy too long," Grandy replied. "What this ranch needs is a strong hand."

Doberman, Vegas and Creel were dead, and their bodies were carried to the barn. They took Bealer there, too, where he was bound securely. Fiske and Lanier, only slightly wounded, were helped to the house, where Syl did what she could for them.

Grandy had gone back to his room. Jeff had had a brief talk with him, but hadn't asked many questions because he had seemed tired. Syl was able to tell him a little about what had happened. She had been caught by Lanier again and tied up once more. Then, when Lanier had gone outside after the men got back, Grandy had come to her room.

"I couldn't believe it when I saw him," she said. "He looked like he was going to die the next step he took, but his hands were steady and his voice was like it used to be. He said if a man's heart went bad but didn't kill him right away he had a chance to build back. He started before you got back, exercising at night. He took it very easy at first."

"And no one guessed?"

"Only Doc Hyman. Grandy swore him to secrecy. He knew what he was up against. He's had a gun in his bed for days, but to kill Doberman wasn't enough. He had to be strong enough to face the others, so he waited."

"He could have sent a message to Dan, or Nels, or someone like that. The doctor would have done it for him."

"If he had done that, and men had come to his rescue, some of them would have been killed. It was his problem. He wanted to handle it his own way. And, for a time, he did have a man to depend on. Andy Culp. But after Andy was killed he had no one."

Wade came in while Syl was talking. "I didn't know Andy was killed," he said defensively. "If I'd known the truth, I'd have booted Doberman off the ranch."

Jeff stared down at his hands and was silent. But not Syl. Someone had to answer Wade, and she took it on herself. "Wade," she said quietly.

"Say that again. Say it loudly, so we can hear it. What would you have done to Matt Doberman? And how would you have done it?"

He couldn't meet her eyes. He looked at Jeff, then looked away. His mouth started working, and his neck got red, the color creeping up into his cheeks.

"I wouldn't say much if I were you," Syl continued. "I'm going to try to remember you're my brother. My little brother, who hasn't grown up."

But Wade couldn't take it like this. He had to hit back. A rush of anger making him reckless, he waved his arm as though to brush away all she had said. "At least I didn't marry an outlaw. That's one thing."

Syl smiled. "He's my husband. Shall I tell him what you called him?"

Wade backed away, turned and left the room, and a few minutes later they heard his horse racing away. They didn't know, then, that he was leaving the Park. Abe Waldron would tell them the next day that Wade had stopped there on the way to the pass and told them, bitterly, that with Jeff back he wasn't necessary, that he would make his fortune on his own, and that someday he would return. And it might happen that way.

The posse rode in an hour later. Dan Hotchkiss, Nels Gitterhaul and half a dozen others were with the sheriff, and the next half hour belonged to Grandy. Everyone wanted to see him, and no one questioned him when he summed up the situation by saying he had been sick and a prisoner in his own home. "If I'd recognized Jeff as my son, he'd have been killed. Wade's a good boy, but he's young. Syl's a woman. Wasn't much I could do but wait until I got well."

That took care of the major problem, but then Grandy said one more thing. "You fellows know Brick Rawson, don't you?"

The sheriff nodded. "Sure we do."

"A fine young man," Grandy said. "He's my daughter's husband. Maybe one of these days I'll be a grandfather."

Syl fixed a light meal for the posse. While she was doing this, the sheriff questioned Bealer, Fiske and Lanier. In another part of the house, Jeff had a brief talk with Dan and Nels. He felt he was doing a bad job of thanking them, but they seemed to understand. Then he went outside, found Brick and told him where he was going. A few minutes later he was riding back to town.

It was a long trip, and it should have tired him—but it didn't. When he got to Crestline and turned down the street, it felt good to ride along and not worry about danger lurking in the shadows.

Although it was late, there was a light in the

Sennett home. He knocked, and Gwen opened the door.

She stepped quickly back as he came in, and she stared at him, her arms stiffly at her sides.

"I came soon as I could," Jeff said.

Her words were low. "It seemed like a long time."

"But I'm here now. It's all over. Do you want to hear?"

"Not now. Jeff, why have you come?"

He was smiling. "Don't you know? I've come for you."

"Then why are you waiting?"

He stepped forward, raising his arms, and Gwen met him halfway. And it was like being home, only much finer than that. He wanted to shout, and he wanted to whisper. He wanted to laugh, and to cry. He wanted to be rough, and he wanted to be tender. And all that would happen.

Mrs. Sennett looked in from the bedroom. She stood watching them for a time, then wisely closed the door and left them alone.

Center Point Large Print
600 Brooks Road / PO Box 1
Thorndike, ME 04986-0001 USA

(207) 568-3717

US & Canada:
1 800 929-9108
www.centerpointlargeprint.com